DEATH IN
THE DARKNESS

She came to the path and pushed her way through the hole in the hedge. Once in the overgrown garden she stood still, turning her flashlight this way and that, hearing, with faint uneasiness, the creak and scrape of the ancient elms above her.

She halted, thinking that someone had called out. "It was only the wind," she said aloud, and laughed a little to reassure herself. Not completely confident, she turned off the light. What its beam did most successfully, she thought, was to make her position obvious to—whoever had called out. That is, if anyone had called.

Suddenly the blood chilled in her veins. Close by her, almost at her feet it seemed, had come a groan, a low sighing groan of one as much in sorrow as in pain.

BANTAM BOOKS offers the finest in classic and modern English murder mysteries. Ask your bookseller for the books you have missed.

Agatha Christie

DEATH ON THE NILE
A HOLIDAY FOR MURDER
THE MOUSETRAP AND OTHER PLAYS
THE MYSTERIOUS AFFAIR AT STYLES
POIROT INVESTIGATES
POSTERN OF FATE
THE SECRET ADVERSARY
THE SEVEN DIALS MYSTERY
SLEEPING MURDER

Carter Dickson

DEATH IN FIVE BOXES

Catherine Aird

HENRIETTA WHO?
HIS BURIAL TOO
A LATE PHOENIX
A MOST CONTAGIOUS GAME
PARTING BREATH
PASSING STRANGE
THE RELIGIOUS BODY
SLIGHT MOURNING
SOME DIE ELOQUENT
THE STATELY HOME MURDER

Patricia Wentworth

MISS SILVER COMES TO STAY
SHE CAME BACK

Elizabeth Lemarchand

BURIED IN THE PAST
DEATH ON DOOMSDAY

Margaret Erskine

CASE WITH THREE HUSBANDS
THE FAMILY AT TAMMERTON
HARRIET FAREWELL
NO. 9 BELMONT SQUARE
THE WOMAN AT BELGUARDO

Margaret Yorke

CAST FOR DEATH
DEAD IN THE MORNING
GRAVE MATTERS

Margery Allingham

BLACK PLUMES
DANCERS IN MOURNING
TETHER'S END
TRAITOR'S PURSE

Elizabeth Daly

THE BOOK OF THE CRIME
EVIDENCE OF THINGS SEEN
THE WRONG WAY DOWN

E. X. Ferrars

MURDERS ANONYMOUS

S. T. Haymon

DEATH AND THE PREGNANT VIRGIN

HARRIET FAREWELL

Margaret Erskine

BANTAM BOOKS
TORONTO · NEW YORK · LONDON · SYDNEY

All the characters in this book are fictitious, and any
resemblance to actual persons, living or dead, is purely coincidental.

*This low-priced Bantam Book
has been completely reset in a type face
designed for easy reading, and was printed
from new plates. It contains the complete
text of the original hard-cover edition.*
NOT ONE WORD HAS BEEN OMITTED.

HARRIET FAREWELL

*A Bantam Book / published by arrangement with
Doubleday and Company Inc.*

PRINTING HISTORY

*Doubleday edition published July 1975
Bantam edition / March 1984*

ISBN 0-553-23780-2

Published simultaneously in the United States and Canada

---

*Bantam Books are published by Bantam Books, Inc. Its trade-
mark, consisting of the words "Bantam Books" and the por-
trayal of a rooster, is Registered in U.S. Patent and Trademark
Office and in other countries. Marca Registrada. Bantam
Books, Inc., 666 Fifth Avenue, New York, New York 10103.*

PRINTED IN THE UNITED STATES OF AMERICA

O   0 9 8 7 6 5 4 3 2 1

HARRIET
FAREWELL

Chapter One

Emma, youngest of Theodore Buckler's three daughters-in-law, came hurrying through the woods, scuffling up the gold-brown leaves as she walked.

She was a tall, lanky girl. She wore a well-fitting pair of blue denim trousers and a short tartan coat. A bright red hat like a small upturned bucket was tipped forward over her short nose. Her very fine hair was worn in a bun from which it perpetually escaped.

She stepped into the open. She halted, looking across the grass sweep of the narrow valley to where, in the thin sunlight of a November morning, her father-in-law's house stood, pale and symmetrical in its classic beauty. Not that Theodore could claim any credit for its appearance. When he had bought it shortly after the Second World War it had been standing there for more than two hundred years.

The summer had been dry and dull, the autumn free from frosts. The trees were still thick with leaves and the flower beds very gay with roses, chrysanthemums and marguerites. The sky was a soft, cloudless blue. It

1

was, Emma mused, taking deep breaths, a morning on which it was good to be alive.

She ran down the long slope, skirting the edge of the lake. She came to a painted iron seat. Here another of the Buckler wives was sitting. Small, slight, she sat very still, wrapped in a dark blue cloak, the hood of which had been pushed back.

Her head was tilted. She gave the impression of listening with an air of strained attention to something that was being said. Only she was quite alone.

It was just a year and seven months since her little boy had been killed in a motor accident. Just under six weeks since she had come out of a mental home.

"Hullo, Harriet! Have you had any breakfast?" Emma asked.

"No." Harriet did not look up as she spoke. Her voice was dull and flat.

"Come and have it with us." Emma added cheerfully, "I have a feeling that I'm late again. If you're there, it will stop Geoffrey bawling me out. Besides, you must get tired of looking at the lake."

"Not tired," Harriet answered. "Just sad. I know there is something I ought to remember. Yet when I listen I hear only a confusion of voices."

Emma nodded. Depressive psychosis. The words formed automatically in her mind but they meant little. To her warm, friendly nature this sister-in-law was not a case but a human being in distress. During the time that had elapsed since Harriet had come home, a kind of friendship had grown up between them.

"What sort of message? I mean—I hope it's a nice one."

Harriet sighed deeply. "I never get *nice* messages." Her eyes returned to their contemplation of the still water. "When I get this one I shall know what to do."

Emma did not like the sound of this but she knew from experience that it was useless to pursue one topic for long. She said, "Don't forget that there's a party here tonight. I shall be looking out for you."

"Will Consuelo be there?" This was Theodore's third wife.

"Yes, but it's not her party. It's Dad's." Since Emma had called her own father by his Christian name, it had been easy enough for her to adopt her husband's mode of address for her father-in-law.

"Consuelo said things that weren't true." Harriet raised her ravaged face to Emma's, fear in her eyes. "They couldn't have been true, could they?" Although she had thrown off a knowledge that had been too heavy to be borne and could not now recall what it had been, some part of her mind remembered, Emma reflected, albeit in an obscure and disordered form.

"Of course they weren't true," Emma assured her. "Consuelo just says these things. You mustn't take any notice." But Harriet had forgotten Emma's presence. She was listening again, with the same air of almost painful attention. Listening for the message that, it was hoped by most of the family, would never get through to her.

Emma stifled a sigh. She set out for her own home, a charming modern house, wedding present from Theodore to his youngest son. As she opened the front door she was met by a rush of warm air and the reassuring smell of grilled kippers.

She pulled off her hat and cast it down. She turned into the pleasant green and white dining room. Here Geoffrey Buckler, a tall studious-looking young man, was reading the morning newspaper.

"Sorry I'm late." Emma embraced her husband warmly. "I was helping William and Ben sort out the fireworks for tonight."

Geoffrey solemnly unwound the scarf. When it was gone he pushed aside the soft, untidy hair at the nape of her neck and kissed her. "My skinny wife, do you realise that you are twenty-five minutes late?"

"Oh, no! Not as much as that." Emma was conscience-stricken. "I don't know where the time goes—" She stopped speaking. Her body stiffened in his arms.

"What?" she demanded in the tones of a Lady Macbeth, "what is that?"

Geoffrey looked round, peering through his large, horn-rimmed spectacles to see what it was that had so affected his wife. "Oh, that! It's a hot plate," he said amiably. "Don't know why we didn't think of buying one. The kippers look just as if they were fresh from the grill."

Emma detached herself from his arms. Sank into her chair. "That bloody, bloody woman!" she cried furiously. "How I hate her."

Geoffrey looked at her. "We're not going to have all that again, are we?" he asked with a mildly rueful air.

"Yes, we are," Emma cried hotly. "We've been married for over a year. For the last five months we've been living here. And practically every week of those five months Consuelo has interfered in my life." She gave an angry laugh. "Consuelo! Why should I have to call her that, as if we were friends?"

"It does happen to be her name. And, since none of us wanted to call her Mother, it seemed a sensible solution." Geoffrey's air of sweet reasonableness and calm common sense did nothing to appease his wife. He added humorously, "Consuelo is a woman of little imagination. She can't believe that we really prefer a life of ups and downs. Of sudden emergencies and shattering crises. Hence these aids to conventional living. And you must admit that Dora was a find. She's a jolly good cook and a hard worker."

Emma glowered. "She's a spy."

"In the pay of the Russians, no doubt." Geoffrey's temper was becoming a little frayed.

"In the pay of your mother-in-law. Everything that happens here is passed on to Consuelo almost as soon as it takes place. I know because when we meet she brings it up and in such a mean, snaky way that I can never pin her down and have a good stand-up row."

"For this relief much thanks." Geoffrey sat down at the table and put aside his newspaper, remarking,

"Where Consuelo is concerned you're becoming quite paranoid."

Emma was cut to the heart. "Like Harriet, I suppose."

Geoffrey had regretted his remark almost as soon as he had made it. "Sorry, Emma. That was a stupid thing to say. I apologise."

"And you'll tell Consuelo to stop interfering?"

"Be reasonable. How can I? When she only does these things out of kindness."

"Kind? That describes Consuelo about as accurately as it would a rattlesnake. Oh, I know she always speaks very pleasantly to you, but that is only because she despairs of finding you doing anything disreputable."

"I would have thought that goes for my two half brothers as well."

"How could it? Miles goes on gambling his money away, in spite of anything Dad can say, and James is still determined to build on the far side of the park, out of sight of the house. I saw him this morning. He and Philip Wheatley were up there measuring and poking about."

"Then he's a fool. If he doesn't look out, he may find that Dad has left the property outright to Consuelo."

Emma looked at him aghast. "Oh, no! Geoffrey, couldn't you speak to James? Life here would be absolute hell if Consuelo were in command."

"Emma, how you do exaggerate. And, since I'm a bit tired of the subject, perhaps you'll leave it alone."

Emma stared at him disbelievingly. How could he be so blind? How could he take Consuelo's part? Sit there looking so calm? Buttering toast, removing the backbone from his kipper. It—it was monstrous.

"If that's your last word I won't go on living with you," she burst out. "I won't share you with my mother-in-law."

Geoffrey looked mildly surprised. "Rather an indelicate suggestion, isn't it?"

"I want a divorce."

"You want what?"

"You heard! I want a divorce."

"On what grounds?"

"The—the irreparable breakdown of our marriage. Or whatever the jargon is."

Geoffrey said briskly, "But it hasn't broken down."

"As far as I'm concerned it has. And if you won't ask for a divorce, I shall leave you. After five years apart I can get one for myself."

Five years! Her heart cried out in protest. It was a lifetime. She felt stunned with horror at the thought.

"And how do you propose to keep yourself?" Geoffrey was growing angry too. "Not in any domestic capacity, I trust?"

"I can always support myself as a model. It's what I used to do when my father hadn't sold any of his paintings. But, as it happens, I have had a job offered me. Cedric Carter wants me to work for him. I know I've done it before, but now he has offered to pay me. He's even going to let me make a second Frenchman— or most of it."

Geoffrey made the mistake of laughing—not because he was amused but because he was angry. He was also jealous, although this he did not realise. "Ilverstoke's papier-mâché Madame Tussaud's—not to mention objects that lady never dreamt of. Old boots that are really candlesticks and bloodstained hands on which half-witted girls can keep their trumpery rings. And those awful life-size figures you can buy. The witch in Welsh costume and the Disappearing Frenchman—"

"You're an intellectual snob," Emma cried, glaring at him. "And you don't buy the figures. You only hire them. The witch is for Halloween or to make up a coven. And so many people have hired the Frenchman that he's become a sort of cult hero."

"I suppose your friend didn't, in the interest of business, dispose of the original? He was a real human being, you know. He did come to this country and he did vanish. He even had a name. Justin something or other."

"Everyone knows he never came to Ilverstoke. That was just a story made up by a local policeman. He wanted promotion or something."

"And your friend Cedric sees to it that the poor fellow's indiscretion is not forgotten." Geoffrey laughed again. "He is even going to make—no, forgive me—he is going to let you make a second Disappearing Frenchman."

"It's easy for you to sneer," Emma declared hotly. "You have a rich father who dotes on you. Cedric left school at fifteen and has supported himself ever since."

Said Geoffrey stiffly, "It may surprise you to learn that we live wholly, and not too badly, I think you'll agree, on what I make from my books." He added as he poured himself a cup of coffee, "Since you seem determined to leave, I would be grateful if you would put off your departure until after Dad's birthday."

"I wouldn't dream of going before that. Nor of missing the Guy Fawkes party this evening." Emma felt dazed at the way this quarrel had grown. She wanted above all to make it up. Instead, she heard herself saying haughtily, "I suppose you have no objection to my packing my things, ready to leave the day after tomorrow? I'm sorry that I shall have to wear some of the clothes you bought me. I can't get into mine because I'm still growing." Her voice quavered on the last word. She felt that she was too young for what was happening to her.

Geoffrey hardened his heart. This nonsense about Consuelo must be crushed once and for all. "What's the point of leaving your clothes? I can't see them fitting either Vivian or Harriet."

"They may not fit any other Buckler wife but they're nice clothes. The Red Cross or Oxfam would be pleased to have them." Emma added with immense dignity, "And now everything is settled I'll go upstairs and move my belongings into one of the spare rooms."

Geoffrey threw down his toast. He glared. "No, damn it, you can't do that. I absolutely forbid it."

Emma glared back. "Your father's birthday may have forced me to remain here in person. In spirit I have already left you."

Before Emma could reach the door it was thrown

open. Miles Buckler burst in. This was Harriet's husband and the younger of Theodore's two sons by his first wife. He was of medium height, well-built and athletic-looking. His brown hair had a dark reddish tint which was repeated in the colour of his eyes. As a rule his expression was gay, even raffish. Since the return of Harriet he had worn a harassed and anxious air.

"Hullo, you two," was his greeting. "Emma, don't go. I wanted to ask you whether you've seen Harriet this morning?"

"Yes, not twenty minutes ago," Emma answered. "She was sitting on the seat by the lake."

Miles groaned. "I wish she wouldn't do that. It gives me the creeps." He added gloomily, "Ever since Consuelo upset her she has been so otherworldly it just isn't true."

"I know," said Emma. "And now she's hearing voices."

Miles looked more worried than before. "What sort of voices?"

"Confused voices. She hasn't really made out what they're saying."

"Oh lor'! As long as they don't tell her to drown herself."

"How does she seem when she's with you?" Geoffrey asked.

"That's the point," Miles answered sourly. "She never is with me. When Harriet sees me coming she makes off—usually for the woods. She's afraid of me. And why shouldn't she be, after what I did?"

"What you did was to indulge in a perfectly reasonable outburst. Bunny was your son. And Harriet *was* to blame for his death," said Geoffrey.

Miles shook his head. He looked tired and defeated. "Who was I to dispense blame? Even now I drive my car too fast, just as Harriet used to do." He added in a low voice, "No, I was the one who sent her round the twist. Nothing can alter that. And when I think of her as she used to be—" His voice trailed miserably away.

"Snap out of it, Miles," Geoffrey advised. "Come on, stop worrying and have a cup of coffee."

"You can have my kippers too," said Emma. "I shan't be wanting them." She left the room.

Miles stared at the door closing behind her. "What's the matter with the child bride?"

"Emma's got some bee in her bonnet—all nonsense of course—concerning Consuelo."

"So that's it. I wondered how much longer she'd stand our mischief-making mother-in-law."

"What do you mean? *You* wondered."

"Come off it, Geoffrey. You must have noticed that Consuelo has had her knife into Emma from the day she first saw her."

Said Geoffrey stiffly, "It's certainly news to me."

Miles shook a commiserating head. "My poor dumb friend! Hasn't it ever occurred to you that Emma has taken Harriet's place in Dad's affection? Consuelo now has a second rival—and one less than half her age."

It was Geoffrey's turn to stare. "But she always speaks of Emma so kindly."

Miles wagged his head. "Wait until the night of the long knives. Consuelo hates the lot of us, but Emma will be the first to fall. However, I didn't come to talk about that. I came to ask if either of you had seen Harriet. I seem to have my answer to that and a fat lot of good it is going to do me."

"What did you want her for?"

"She has taken something of mine and I want it back."

"Something you value, then?"

"I'm not going to tell you what it is," said Miles darkly. "That way you can keep your peace of mind."

"As bad as that, is it? It begins to look as if it were a mistake to have brought her back."

Miles sighed wearily. "It was Dad who was so keen on the idea. And Harriet did seem to have forgotten the past. At least, she had forgotten until that woman got at her. Now she half remembers." He rose to his feet. "If we get safely through the birthday celebrations, I'll make some other arrangement. Get Harriet a nurse companion." He laughed without humour. "Settle them somewhere where the only water comes out of the tap."

Left alone, Geoffrey went into his workroom. He did not take seriously Emma's demand for a divorce. Such a thing was unthinkable, but he was more shaken than he would have cared to admit by his half brother's view of Consuelo. He determined to speak to her, explaining his dilemma.

He took the cover off his typewriter and began to work.

Emma, standing at the head of the stairs, heard its busy clicking. So Geoffrey was not coming upstairs to end their quarrel. He did not care that she proposed leaving him. She thought despairingly that at eighteen her life was over.

She turned and went into their bedroom, the tears starting from her eyes. Carefully, mournfully, she began to pack away her clothes, putting black tissue paper between each frock. Tucking in newspaper to keep out moths. Her fur coats followed and the jewel case which had been her pride.

Her tears dripped. Her mind reverted to the French village of Collioure on the Côte Vermeille and to the day when Geoffrey, driving a sports Mercedes-Benz, had arrived in search of local colour for a book.

He had stayed so long that, in the end, no one had believed in the book but only that the Englishman was in love with the young Emma Hastings.

Sighing, she recalled those days. Savoured again the mingled scent of geraniums and of the anchovies which, caught locally, were salted away in barrels by the old women of the district.

In October her father had died. He had left neither money nor relations to whom she could have gone. Geoffrey, twelve years her senior, had put aside his scruples about baby-snatching and the disparity of their ages. They had been married on her seventeenth birthday. For eight months they had wandered through France, blissfully happy, her grief for her father assuaged by her love for her husband.

And now it was all over.

Wiping away her tears with the back of her hand, she shrugged herself into her tartan jacket. She let herself out of the house and set out for the Workshop.

It was an ugly semibungalow of grey stone with a slate roof. Its looks were not improved by the bars at every downstairs window. It had three rooms on the ground floor and a single large attic above. It was up to date in that it had water laid on and central heating. Here Cedric Carter tried out new designs and here he brought wholesale buyers to see the stock. What had begun as a gimmick with an ephemeral appeal had been seized on enthusiastically by the young and had grown into a sizable, if eccentric, business.

The first room with its walls covered in a dull black material hanging in heavy folds, its ceiling draped to resemble a tent, the squat white leather chairs, the frosted glass windows, all added up to a strangely claustrophobic atmosphere.

Open shelf fittings were lighted to give the maximum eerie effect to a collection that included voodoo masks, monster eyeballs, sinister alley cats, great clumps of ostrich feathers and the objects mentioned by Geoffrey. In one corner sat the Welsh Witch, a cat and a toad at her feet.

Behind this room was a smaller one, uncluttered and very light, used by Cedric and Emma as a workroom. The third and smallest room was narrow and dingy. Here the papier-mâché figures, which could be hired out, were kept. In the attic was the main body of the stock.

Emma tried the front door. It opened, so she knew that Cedric was there. He was slim, voluble and lively. He had large sympathetic brown eyes and an agile mind. He dressed in a very trendy manner. He was, to their mutual amusement, exactly the same height as Emma.

He stood now in the front room, arranging a series of differing-sized mugs of which the handles appeared to be five curled pink toes. "You've been crying," he said, seemingly without looking at her.

"That's Consuelo," said Emma, taking off her coat. She looked at the mugs. "What revolting ideas you do get, Cedric."

"But paying ones." Cedric added, "I've told you before that if you made up your mind just to accept the things she gives you, she'd soon stop sending them."

Emma sighed. "It's too late for that. This morning I said that I was going to leave Geoffrey."

"What did he say to that?"

"He said he'd be obliged if I'd put it off until after Dad's birthday."

"The monster." Cedric stood back to admire his work. "Never mind. You can always come here to live. We could fix up part of the top floor." He added, "Consuelo wasn't trying to get a rise out of her sons-in-law. Never think it. She's a hot-blooded Latin. Nothing but their utter ruin will satisfy her."

Emma was used to Cedric's dramatic pronouncements. Now she said, prosaically, "Consuelo would find it awfully hard to ruin someone who had Dad on their side and almost unlimited money."

"Ah, money!" cried Cedric. "How I worship it. But come into the next room. I've set up the wire frame for the body of the second Frenchman. I've ordered his clothes and I had a bit of luck with the faded puce-coloured beret. I saw one on a junk stall and bought it for three new pence."

Emma looked at the figure of the original Frenchman with distaste. "Are you going to give him the same expression?" She always thought of the dummy as "him," never as "it."

"If I can manage it. It's the way his eyes seem to follow one about with a look of furtive malignity that makes him so successful. In the midst of their festivities it gives people what you would call a '*frisson*.'"

"I can't bear catching his eye, but then I don't feel happy turning my back on him either."

"There's nothing to prevent you putting him away with the others."

Emma was delighted with this suggestion. "Why

didn't I think of that? When I don't want him as a pattern I'll put him in the back room."

Cedric looked at her solemnly. "What's the betting you won't imagine that you can hear him moving about?"

With a pestle Emma had been pulping up some shredded newspaper immersed in water in a small bath. She turned. "Cedric Carter, you are the most abominable man. I've a good mind to throw this nasty mixture over you."

Cedric put his arms up in a mock protective gesture. "Or perhaps as you pass you'll hear a slight creak as he flexes his limbs."

"That settles it," Emma cried, half laughing, half alarmed. "Nothing would induce me to sleep here. I'd just lie awake all night thinking that I heard him on the stairs."

"Exactly! Creak, thump. Creak, thump." Cedric burst out laughing. He gave her a sly glance. "Never mind. You can always come and live with me."

Geoffrey had luncheon alone. The meal over, he walked across to the big house in search of his step-mother. He asked Grant, the butler, where he would find her and was told that she was in the parlour. The room had been designated thus in the original plans of the house. The name had stuck. It had always been a pleasant room. Now it was beautiful, for Consuelo had both the taste and the money to indulge it, even without recourse to her husband.

For her it was a workroom. Here she went through the weekly housekeeping accounts. Planned the meals and interviewed the cook. Dictated letters to her social secretary.

Geoffrey knocked on the door. There followed a silence. A silence so prolonged that he was just about to conclude that Grant had been wrong, when Consuelo spoke.

"Who is it?" Her voice was high, startled.

"Geoffrey." He heard a drawer open and close.

"Come in."

He opened the door. Consuelo was standing with her back to the French ormolu desk at which she worked. One hand rested on it as if for support, the other was pressed to her heart. There was a bright patch of colour on each cheek.

Her eyes were wide and dilated. She was breathing in quick shallow gasps.

"Don't you feel well?" Geoffrey asked, a note of concern in his voice.

"Quite well. At least—yes, perhaps I do feel a little strange." She sank into the straight-backed chair, feeling for it with one hand stretched out behind her.

Geoffrey looked round the room. A decanter and some wineglasses stood on a silver tray. He poured out a drink.

"Take this. It's only sherry but it should stop you feeling faint."

"Thank you." Consuelo gulped it down. She managed a smile, a meaningless stretching of her lips. "I feel quite well again." She rested her forehead in her hand for a moment, eyes closed. When she opened them she smiled at him, her usual warm smile. "I suppose I have been doing too much, but then I always want my parties to be a credit to your father. What can I do for you?"

"It's about my wife." The use of the word wife seemed, to his mind, to bind Emma more closely to him.

Consuelo laughed, a shrill, reckless sound that shocked Geoffrey because it seemed misplaced. "Emma, so young, so bohemian. So ignorant in social matters. What can I do for her?"

"I think it would be best if you left her to her youth and ignorance," said Geoffrey dryly. Adding, "I have only just discovered that she looks on herself as inadequate. That the presents you have been kind enough to give us, in her eyes only accentuate her sense of failure."

"Failure?" Consuelo dropped her lids. She drew out

the word in a meditative way. "I thought your marriage was such a successful one. So happy. So gay."

"So did I. Until today I had no idea that Emma's feelings were so strong. She has threatened to leave me."

"You shock me," said Consuelo—but not before a sly smile of triumph had twitched the corners of her lips.

So Consuelo *had* known. Emma had been right there.

"It shocked me," Geoffrey retorted. "So no more presents, please." He decided that it would give him great pleasure to sack the maid, Dora, when she turned up for work next morning.

"Do not ask me to take my presents back, Geoffrey. It would upset your father. And I am determined never to do that again." Consuelo rose to her feet to indicate that the discussion was over. "Do not worry about the young Emma. You have only to go on being uncomfortable and ill-fed and she will not leave you." Her smile was openly derisive. Her eyes full of malice.

Geoffrey thought about it as he crossed the hall. He had been shown—deliberately, he felt—Consuelo's true feelings towards Emma. The mask had been dropped. But why? Thinking back, he connected it somehow with the sound of the closing drawer. What had she secreted there?

We shall know soon enough, he thought—and was conscious of an unusual feeling of foreboding.

He opened the door of the library. His father was sitting where he could look out of one of the long windows, a newspaper open on his knees. He was a handsome man, but Geoffrey's heart smote him, noting again how frail he looked since that wretched upset with Harriet.

"How are you, Dad?" he asked. He put a hand affectionately on Theodore's shoulder. "Not getting too bored, I hope?"

"Not bored at all, my dear boy. Grant's copy of the *Gazette* has reached me in a somewhat roundabout manner. And I manage to keep myself informed of much that happens on the business front." He waved a hand towards a pile of papers on the table at his elbow. "Added to which, sitting here, I can watch a great deal of what goes on outside. Although I must admit some of it makes me sad."

Geoffrey nodded, thinking of the threat poised by Consuelo. "Such as?"

"This morning I saw Miles looking for Harriet. And I saw her run into the woods to avoid him."

"It's a pity it was Miles who told her that Bunny was dead."

"As it turns out, yes. Yet he was the obvious choice. How were we to know that somewhere in her subconscious mind she would remember and resent the things he said to her." Theodore sighed, then smiled. "I also saw Emma. That is always a pleasant sight. I suppose she was going to the Workshop?"

"Yes, she's helping Cedric Carter make another dummy Frenchman. The old one has proved so popular with the students of West Ilverstoke and with the trendy young that it's beginning to show signs of wear."

Theodore laughed. "Emma is an original and independent young thing. You chose well there." His face sobered. "As for the Frenchman, who is it, I wonder, who is determined that he shall not be forgotten? It worries me." He picked up the copy of the Ilverstoke *Gazette*. "Listen, I'll read it to you. *'In memory of Justin Besson, born at Rennes, 2 February 1903. Disappeared 3 April 1973. Not forgotten.'* What do you think of that?"

Geoffrey looked at Theodore affectionately. Since his father's health had become so precarious he had taken to fretting about all kinds of things, although few of them as pointless as this.

"I don't think much of it because I'm pretty certain that the whole saga of the Disappearing Frenchman is the invention of Cedric Carter. As for those dates, if I'd been in this country at the time of Besson's disappearance I bet I should have seen them in the national newspapers, as Cedric must have done. To him it's all good business. He doesn't mean the story to die."

Theodore smiled. "A plausible young man. I suppose that is how he managed to talk me into letting him rent the house in the woods." His smile faded. His gaze had returned to the *In Memoriam* columns of last Friday's local newspaper. The troubled look was back on his face.

Chapter Two

Septimus Finch had been annoyed at having been seconded to Ilverstoke. This somnolent corner, some six miles northwest of the City of London, found no favour in his eyes. Mink-coat land, he called it. Although when he saw the daily State Board he had to admit that the police there were shorthanded.

Of three inspectors and eight sergeants:

One inspector and two sergeants were in hospital after the smashup of the car in which they had been travelling.

One sergeant was on a promotion course.

One inspector was on weekly leave.

One sergeant was with the Divisional Vice Squad.

Of forty-two police constables twenty-one were off for various reasons.

Yes, they were shorthanded all right.

Finch had been assiduous in his enquiries after the health of the invalids, and now Bodkin had just broken it to him that the inspector whose place he had taken had gone on ten days' sick leave.

Finch looked sadly across to where the Superintendent sat, a corpulent man with a high colour, several rolls of fat above his coat collar, and a boisterous manner. There was a cup of coffee in front of him. Every now and then he felt in the drawer of his desk and popped a small iced cake into his mouth.

"It's no good your expecting anything violent to happen here," Bodkin said. He was amused at the aura of gloom that hung over this large, sleepy-looking man. "Financial chicanery is our usual fare. At one time or another we've had some pretty large frauds on our hands. In fact, I dare say this division has had more fraud cases than any other—bar the City."

"Fraud is not in my line," Finch admitted. He sighed faintly. He wished he could leave the Superintendent to get on with his own special subject while he, Finch, returned to New Scotland Yard and the Murder Squad.

"Well, what else can we offer you?" Bodkin affected to think, half closing his eyes so that they were almost lost in the surrounding fat. "How about a disappearing Frenchman? Although I must say that after eighteen months or more, it's not likely that he'll be found."

Finch was interested. "What was the Frenchman doing here?"

"That we shall never know. He came from near Rennes in Brittany. A man of no vices. No financial difficulties. A recluse, shutting himself away from the world. A craftsman, spending his days carving in ivory, for which he had quite an international reputation."

Finch sat bolt upright. "*That* Frenchman!" He beamed at the Superintendent. Or was it at some delectable picture his own mind had conjured up? "I remember. Interpol asked us to find him. He was traced to Victoria Station, where he had arrived by the Boat Train at 10:58 A.M. There the trail ended—or so I thought."

Bodkin chuckled. "Ask Sergeant Hollis," he advised. "But don't believe all he tells you."

The sergeant was a dark, morose-looking man for whom life had turned sour. Everything that could possibly go wrong had gone wrong. He could not imagine what the Yard man wanted of him. Except for his ordinary duties, no one ever did want anything of him.

Glumly he walked along the corridor and knocked.

"Come in." The voice was clear, soft, almost womanish, but there was nothing feminine about the speaker's broad shoulders and lean flanks. Nor in the resolute chin and firm mouth, masked as they were by their owner's habitual air of indolent good nature. "Oh, it's you, Hollis." Finch tipped back his chair until it rested on two legs. "Superintendent Bodkin told me to ask you about the Frenchman who disappeared some eighteen months ago."

To Finch's surprise, Hollis turned a dark red. His mouth drew into a narrow bitter line. "What aspect of the incident are you interested in, sir?" he asked almost insolently.

Finch looked at him curiously. "What ails you, man?"

"Nothing, sir."

"I think there had better be. I ask a question in good faith and you stiffen up and look as if I'd insulted your sainted mother."

Hollis looked embarrassed, a little bewildered. "Sorry, sir. I thought you were at it too."

Finch sighed. "My patience," he pointed out, "is not inexhaustible."

"No, sir. It's just that nothing has gone right for me since the morning when I reported having seen Justin Besson. At first it was thought that I had invented the incident, hoping that it would help me to rise to inspector. I was ambitious in those days, believing that my career was going well. Besides, I'd just got married."

"I think I saw you with your wife. A very pretty fair girl." And both of you looking as melancholy as pallbearers, Finch thought. He said aloud, "What went wrong?"

"Suddenly the whole thing became a joke. From being something rather discreditable on my part, it became wildly funny. Here, in the local, in shops even, every one was sniggering. Even now, if anything is lost, someone is certain to say 'Ask Hollis', or, 'It's gone with the Frenchman and no one knows where that is, except Hollis.' "

Finch nodded. "Interesting," he drawled. "Very interesting. Proceed."

Hollis paled. "Does that mean, sir, that you think I may have seen this Frenchman?" he asked incredulously.

"Why not? As the Good Book says, some shall have the gift of tongues. Some that of prophecy. Why shouldn't you have a gift for faces?" Finch's gently murmuring voice ran on. "You wouldn't be the only one. Although in these degenerate days most of them find themselves in the Special Branch rather than in the arena with the lions."

"I've had a bellyful of the lions," Hollis muttered.

"Forget them," Finch told him. "Concentrate on this missing man. Otherwise we'll never find out where he got to." Adding happily, "For wherever it was he seems to have stayed there."

"I did think—" said Hollis, then broke off.

"Let's get back to the beginning. To when you saw the Frenchman."

Hollis took a deep breath. He still looked slightly dazed, unable to believe in this change in his fortunes. "As you probably know already, Justin Besson came to this country on an Easter Monday twelve months ago last April. It was the day of the fair that has been held here every year since the reign of the first Elizabeth. I was very keen on my job then and, with what seemed like half London making for the common, I kept a sharp lookout for any villains, pick-pockets, con-men and the like. It wasn't until a week later when a photograph of a missing Frenchman was circulated to all police stations in the metropolitan area that I realised I'd seen the man walking up Grove Drive." He added bitterly, "It wasn't a face to forget but no one would believe that I could have remembered one person in all that crowd."

"But there must have been some follow-up?"

"Very little, sir, for—for reasons I've already explained."

"And Grove Drive? What kind of district is that?"

"Entirely residential. It's a wide road with plenty of

traffic. On one side there are a number of large handsome houses, standing in their own grounds. And now all but one converted into flats. On the other there's just this one property. Westlea Park, it's called, home of a Mr. Theodore Buckler."

"Of the property-development company?"

"Yes, sir. Although at one time you'd have associated the name with a shipping line. Theodore Buckler is said always to have kept one jump in front of the market. He made a first fortune from shipping and sold out before the slump."

"And you've traced some connection between your Frenchman and this Mr. Buckler?"

Hollis looked worried, uncertain once more. "I don't know about that, sir. At first I picked on a fellow called Cedric Carter. For the last two years he has rented a stone building on the Westlea Park estate. And before that he had a stall in one of these open-air antique markets, so I thought he had the right connections, particularly as he had been selling a fraudulent line in scrimshaw—which I understand is a fanciful design etched on whales' teeth and tusks, done originally by whalers in the old days."

"And that led nowhere?"

"I decided not." Hollis explained Cedric Carter's present occupation. "I thought that if he'd been responsible for Besson's disappearance he would hardly have called attention to himself by making an effigy of him. Besides, there was something I didn't know at first. If the Frenchman had been going to meet Carter he would have turned off Grove Drive into the woods some way before getting to where I saw him."

Finch nodded. "I think I like your last reason best."

"Yes, sir? Well, I came on the second lead quite by chance. Finding myself at a loss, I thought I'd read up about carving ivory, hoping I might find some clue there. And so I did, but not in the way I had intended. One evening when I went into the library the head librarian was there. When he saw the books I had brought back he said that I should ask Mr. Theodore

Buckler of Westlea Park to show me his fourteenth-century carved 'Annunciation.' He said Mr. Buckler had quite a collection of antique carved ivory but that was his best piece."

"And you went to Westlea Park?"

"No, sir. I transferred my interest to Mr. Buckler and his family."

Finch raised an eyebrow. "Many of them, are there?"

"Not as many as you might have expected, seeing that Mr. Theodore has been married three times. By his first wife he had the two sons, James and Miles. She was a bit of a terror. She drank and gambled, was arrogant and had a temper. She took Theodore to the cleaners before she would agree to divorce him. When that was done she bought herself a large estate in the Bahamas where, if her goings on are anything like they were here, she must startle the natives. Theodore Buckler's next wife was a schoolteacher, a bluestocking but with a zest for life. She died leaving one son, Geoffrey, who is the old man's favourite. Then, about four years ago, while travelling for his health, Mr. Theodore met and married the widow of a rich South American. She's a nice-looking lady, very charming, but not so nice to work for. The staff say if a spot of grease is cleaned away, she wants to know where it has gone. She has no children either by her present husband nor by her first. Lastly there is a nephew. The son of Theodore Buckler's sister. He is the company secretary."

"What sort of men are the sons?"

"Mr. James has taken his father's place on the Board. He's as sharp as his father and a great deal fonder of money. He married an heiress, a plain, stringy-looking woman. They have three children, all away at boarding school. Mr. James and his father occasionally fall out, but Mr. James always comes to heel because he's afraid an open split might damage his prospects.

"The second son, Miles Buckler, is in the firm too but he's a lightweight and something of a playboy. He drives a racing car, goes in for winter sports, and has never been known to refuse a bet or a chase. His father is forever paying his debts. He's patient with him because he reckons he did him a bad turn giving him the mother he did. A matter of genes, you might say, with Mr. Miles more sinned against than sinning."

"Well, it's an original thought. Continue."

"Mr. Miles has a very pretty young wife, Harriet. At least she used to be pretty. They lived with their child, a two-year-old son known as Bunny, in a Victorian house on the estate. Harriet, who was apt to drive her car too fast, had acquired an American Mustang, a car with a left-hand drive. And, one day, twelve months ago last March, she was motoring with the little boy on the seat beside her. She pulled out from behind a lorry, meaning to overtake it, when she saw a large furniture van coming towards her. She kept her head, put her foot down hard on the accelerator and nearly made it. Instead of a head-on crash the van just grazed the car, slicing away one side—and taking the little boy with it. She couldn't get over the shock nor her sense of guilt. She went straight from the hospital to a mental home, from which she emerged only six weeks ago."

Finch had listened, fascinated. Now he tipped his chair back until it swung on one leg. "Had she schizophrenia?"

"No, sir. Amnesia, depression and suicidal tendencies—but not schizophrenia." Hollis, looking at Finch, had a new worry. What was the correct thing to do when one's superior falls flat on his back, as seemed likely at any moment in the Chief Inspector's case.

"But—eighteen months, was it? Only schizos stay in as long as that. A slightly bent doctor seems indicated."

"Well, sir, the place changed hands recently, and she returned home."

"More honest hands evidently," Finch commented in his soft drawling voice. The chair was back on two legs.

"So it would seem, sir. Although at one time the patient herself refused to come home. The very idea threw her into what, I understand, is called 'a state of withdrawal.'"

"Does she remember what had happened?"

"The general opinion is that she does not."

Hollis had been speaking quite animatedly. Finch looked at him with amusement. "And where did you get all your information?"

"From Mr. Grant, the butler at Westlea Park," Hollis answered with a grin. "We go to the same public house, sir. I've been cultivating him for the past eighteen months."

"He knows that you are a policeman?"

"Yes, sir. In view of what I intended to be a protracted acquaintanceship I judged it best."

Finch nodded. "Very sensible. And how about Geoffrey Buckler?"

"He's very different from his two half brothers. He's not in the business but is the author of a very popular line in guidebooks. They're an interesting mixture of hard facts, legend and out-of-the-way information."

"Guaranteed to appeal to the intelligentsia as well as to the general public?"

"That's right, sir. Mr. Geoffrey married an English girl who had lived most of her life in France. He brought her back some five months ago. She's very young. Very popular with everyone but Mrs. Buckler, senior, but then that lady doesn't like any of the family. It seems she wants to have her husband to herself."

"But the Frenchman? Could there be any connection between him and Mrs. Geoffrey Buckler?"

"I couldn't find any, sir—except that both were connected with the arts, since Besson was a sculptor and Emma Hastings, as she was before her marriage, was the daughter of a painter, Paul Hastings, an Englishman living in France. And even there the connection is weak, since Besson was successful and Hastings a failure."

"So we are left without any further information as to the fate of the sculptor?"

"That's right, sir—unless you accept that there is a connection between him and what happened to The Elms, Miles Buckler's house, late on the day of Besson's disappearance."

"And what did happen?"

"The Elms caught fire, sir. The house was completely gutted."

A silence followed. Finch broke it.

The chair legs descended with a bang. "Now isn't that gratifying. Hollis, you have made my day."

"You've made mine, sir," said Hollis fervently.

It was Tuesday, November 5. Finch, returning to the police station, made a detour that would take him past the two hundred acres which comprised Westlea Park. He came to the big double gates. They were open, and beyond them he could see a sloping stretch of pasture studded with an occasional tree, with a lake and woods beyond.

Just inside the gates was what might have been described as a large lodge or a small house, the lower windows screened by a hedge from the gaze of anyone passing in the road.

He slowed down to take a longer look—which was as well, since at that moment a woman ran out of the gates and straight in front of the car. He braked and it stopped with the woman resting against the bonnet.

At the same time from within the gates he heard an anguished cry.

"Harriet! For God's sake, take care."

For a moment Harriet Buckler stayed frozen and still. Her eyes were fixed on Finch but her attention was all for the man who had cried out.

She had, Finch saw, the sad remnants of beauty. The pure oval of her face, the large, dark blue and heavily lashed eyes, the delicately chiselled features, all rendered strange and a little dismaying by something fierce and wild in her expression.

Her clothes, too, were odd. She wore no coat but had on an ankle-length black frock of some soft woollen material. It had long sleeves and a rounded neckline. Her dark hair was tied at the nape of her neck with a bow of black ribbon. She wore low-heeled strap shoes on her small feet. Her only ornament was a narrow belt made of fine silver links.

Miles Buckler and Mad Harriet, Finch thought, delighted with his luck. He opened the car door and slid his long legs out. "Are you hurt?" he asked, not moving towards her, for there was in her face a quite desperate determination—to do what? Throw herself under the next passing car? Escape from the good-looking man now coming, white-faced and shaken, through the gateway.

It seemed as if the latter guess was the right one, for, with eyes fixed on him in an unblinking stare, the woman seemed to glide round the bonnet and down the length of the car.

"I thought you'd killed her," Miles Buckler said hoarsely to Finch.

Harriet chose that moment to move. She whisked round the car, through the gates, and sped away up the drive, her skirts flying out like the wings of a crow.

Miles stared after her. "Oh, what's the use?" he muttered.

"You look as if you could do with a drink," said Finch in his soft drawl.

"You'd better join me."

"I'll watch you having one."

"Don't drink and drive? Well, it's a good axiom." He added as he led the way into the house, "I'm Miles Buckler."

"My name is Finch." The Yard man was admiring the small pieces of antique furniture in the hall. He was also wondering why one door had been repainted and not the other three.

"Better come into the dining room," said Miles.

Once there he took a clean cup and saucer from the side table, then indicated two Thermos jugs. "Coffee? Milk? The sugar is in the bowl." He poured himself a stiff whisky and water and stood sipping it, staring moodily out of the windows.

"That was my wife," he said abruptly, "although it's difficult for me to realise. The mental home got her up like that and she seems to have taken a fancy to the garb. I'd have liked her to have been a bit easier on the eye—but then that's the least of my worries."

"She has been in a mental home?" Finch prompted.

"Yes, for the last eighteen months or more." Miles described in a few words the accident that had killed his baby son and injured his wife. "Instead of the sympathy Harriet had the right to expect," he ended, "I bawled her out. The next thing I heard was that she had gone out of her mind and remembered nothing. No, that's not quite correct. She remembers to be afraid of me."

"Your wife is living in this house?"

Miles laughed jarringly. "I suppose you could call it that. Most of the night she is out in the woods and most of the day she is in the grounds somewhere. The doors are never locked so that she can come and go as she pleases. I thought, wrongly as it turned out, that coming to a house she didn't know she'd find no painful associations and would settle down, but it didn't work." He added abruptly, "I burnt down our old home."

"If you're going to say things like that, perhaps I'd better tell you that I am a policeman."

Miles sighed. "I didn't mean that I burnt down the house deliberately. It was just damned carelessness on my part, although at the time I could have sworn that I had turned out the electric fire. I've never forgiven myself. If I hadn't got in the habit of spending most of the day in the boy's nursery—of going out only after dark—" He fell silent, brooding.

"Why after dark?" Finch prompted.

"Because I couldn't bear meeting anyone I knew. And, since I've lived all my life in Ilverstoke, I know an awful lot of people. Anyway, there it was. My brother James had come round to keep me company and I went out for a walk with him. When we got back the whole place had gone up in flames. The house and every last thing in it. Photographs, toys, Bunny's nursery furniture, the Beatrix Potter animals walking round the walls. Everything that had belonged to my son had gone. Everything!" There was genuine anguish in his voice and in his bitter, regretful expression.

"And it was after that you visited your wife in hospital?"

"What? No, I'd already done the damage there. The

doctors tell me she doesn't remember anything. But she must do. Otherwise why does she treat me as if I had horns and a tail?" He was silent a moment. "She won't eat with me but when I'm away in the City she'll come in for a midday meal cooked by the daily woman. Yes, and she'll sit up at table. Over the weekend and after I get back in the evening, she just helps herself to something out of the fridge when she gets hungry. She'll eat it there and then in the kitchen." He laughed drearily. "If I inadvertently go in she retires and finishes her meal in the garden."

"And her condition shows no sign of improving?"

"None. I thought that she'd come to see that I was harmless enough. Instead, being here has made her a great deal more queer than she was before. She—she's becoming quite irrational. Sometimes she even frightens me and then I feel more guilty than ever. Not that I was ever one to enjoy wearing a hair shirt but when one has a wife with suicidal tendencies who spends hours sitting by the side of the lake just staring at the water, one comes to feel pretty desperate."

"Since it has been such a failure, I wonder you haven't made some other arrangement for her."

"It's because of my father. He was very fond of Harriet—and even in her present condition she is drawn to him. He just says give her time. And, as we have been warned not to upset him in any way because of his heart, I'm in a bit of a difficulty."

"Your wife looked in a bit of a difficulty too."

"That's because she—well, she's like a magpie. She keeps taking things out of the house and hiding them away. Mostly it's something bright and—and without value."

"And this time?"

Miles laughed. It had a hollow sound and his eyes were uneasy. "This time she had taken a bronze statuette of our son. I want it back."

"You think she remembers him?"

"I don't know what she— No, of course she doesn't

remember him. It was just that it was bright and—and shining."

Finch left Miles there, drinking and staring out in a discouraged way to where the last of the autumn flowers bloomed, although autumn itself was past. It seemed fitting.

Finch drove slowly, following the high wall. He came to another pair of iron gates, with a small gate close by. There was a curving moss-grown drive beyond and some tall old elms.

He stayed there for a while, half hoping to see the sad entranced figure of Harriet Buckler glide down the overgrown drive.

She did not come.

Westlea Park was ablaze with light. Geoffrey and Emma walked over to it in silence and several feet apart.

Geoffrey, returning home, full of affection, goodwill and the determination to get rid of Dora, had gone up to their bedroom and found that every sign of Emma's presence had vanished.

It had been like a slap in the face.

He had been furious. He had stormed through the house, calling Emma by name and cursing Cedric. From this first active phase he had passed into one of silent anger, made worse by his secret jealousy.

Emma had purposely returned home late to cut to a minimum the pain of seeing one whom she thought of sadly as her ex-husband. Geoffrey's stormy expression she accepted as being a continuation of the disastrous happening of the morning. Confirmation of the fact that he no longer loved her.

She had changed into a suit of honey-coloured suede, worn with a heavy silk shirt blouse in the same shade. It had been a recent present from her father-in-law. She had been delighted with it but had been aghast at the price, roughly four times as much as she had been accustomed to spend on clothes in a whole year.

When she had put it on she had stood in front of the

long mirror, staring at her reflection. It was a beautiful
suit, dashing yet elegant. It deserved a wearer to
match. As she turned away she had reflected mournfully
that Geoffrey would soon be free to find such a one.
Someone who knew all about large dinner parties,
going to the opera and smart night clubs.

Geoffrey gave his overcoat to Grant. Then, with
Emma smiling determinedly, they went into the library,
a white and gold room designed by the Adam brothers.
There Theodore and his wife were welcoming the first
of their guests.

Consuelo was at her best. She had been beautiful as a
young woman. At forty she was still very lovely by
artificial light. She was wearing a brown velvet trouser
suit, cuffed and collared with sable. She looked chic,
perfectly groomed and sparkling with high spirits.

The guests now were arriving in a steady flow. They
all knew each other. Mothers and fathers bringing their
children. Nannies leaving their charges and intending
to return for them later. Most of the parents could
recall when they themselves had attended the fireworks
display with *their* parents. They were contemporaries
of Harriet's. They enquired for her, sighing and shaking
their well-coiffured heads over the answers.

Cedric Carter came prepared to enjoy himself. He
attached himself to Emma and Geoffrey glowered at
them from a distance.

James Buckler arrived with his wife. She was tall and
flat-chested, with an overlong nose. She was well and
appropriately dressed in a frock, the details of which no
one would notice. She was a great committeewoman.
Not because she felt deeply about any cause but because it was one way of meeting the right people.

James had a great look of his father. He was tall and
thin with keen, deep-set eyes and a sardonic expression. He lacked Theodore's broad humanity.

"You look very nice, child," Vivian said approvingly
to Emma. Adding, "I suppose you've heard that Harriet
has surpassed herself. She has got hold of Miles' gun?"

Emma nodded. "Cedric told me. Everyone seems to

know." Her eyes were drawn to the dark window behind her. Where was Harriet? She had looked for her on her way back from the Workshop but had not found her.

"You mean that everyone connected with the *family* knows," James corrected with a thin smile. "Half these people wouldn't have come if they'd known of Harriet's acquisition. However I don't suppose that she will fire at anyone but our stepmama."

"Surely the really important point is that once Harriet has used the gun she will have no inhibitions about using it again," Vivian declared. "The best we can hope for is that she will end by shooting herself. And I hope everyone will remember that James and I were against having her back. It was Miles who insisted—and Dad backed him up."

A tall thin man, very well-dressed, detached himself from the little group surrounding Consuelo. He came towards them, waving a greeting that embraced the four of them. This was Philip Wheatley.

"Consuelo is in terrific form tonight," he remarked. And then, "Emma, you are a picture of elegance and poise."

James looked across the room at his stepmother. "I suppose it is absurd," he remarked, "but I do mistrust Consuelo when she is in high spirits."

"Consuelo," said Vivian acidly, "is probably uplifted by more thoughts designed to restore Harriet to her senses."

"Come now," said Philip, with an easy laugh, "you must admit that she has quite given up her naughty ways. And she always did bring you her problems and consult you on how Uncle Theodore liked things done."

"Consult? That's one way of putting it," said Vivian, raising her thin pencilled eyebrows. "What I noticed was not so much consultation as a probing curiosity."

Still smiling, Philip looked about him. "I was hoping to find Harriet here. Oddly enough I haven't had a chance to speak to her. She seems always on the move."

"Don't try and find her," Vivian advised. "She won't recognise you and I doubt if you'll recognise her."

"Never say it!" Philip cried. "Harriet was the prettiest, wildest, most enchanting creature. Always ready to take a dare or go with Miles on one of his mad ventures. That's how I remember her. And it's the way I mean to go on remembering her."

He moved on. He considered himself a party expert. Prided himself on always knowing whom to speak to and what to say. He looked at his uncle and wondered how much longer he could last.

Cedric took Emma to the dining room in search of the buffet supper. There he left her. He was a serious eater, particularly when someone else was paying for it.

Geoffrey was there, gloomily drinking alone, surrounded by chattering, giggling children. Emma could see that he was aware of her presence by the way he stiffened. He turned away just as she had decided to smile at him.

Well, I suppose I could ask Consuelo to leave us alone, Emma decided gloomily. Abandoning her third oyster *vol-au-vent* and an admirer of fifteen, she went into the hall and asked Grant for her mother-in-law.

"I did see the mistress a short time ago," the butler answered. "She was with Mr. James. They went in the direction of the parlour."

"Thanks, I'll look there." Emma smiled at him, then turned briskly away. Soon, almost against her will, she slackened pace, caught by the magic of the many rooms, flower-decked and lit up for the party.

The doors were open and one room after another shone out, pale, rich and beautiful, for during the three years Consuelo had been mistress of Westlea Park she had redecorated the whole of the ground floor—and much of the first.

Emma had almost reached the parlour, and had paused to sniff appreciatively at a great bowl of pink carnations, when the door opened violently. James Buckler stalked out, his face white with passion. He flung the door to so violently that the sound echoed down the corridor.

Emma was staring after him in astonishment when the door opened again and Consuelo stepped gracefully into the passage. There was a hint of a smile on her lips. Her expression was one of malicious triumph. She saw Emma. Her expression changed. She still smiled but her whole face had stiffened so that the smile no longer had any meaning—even to herself.

"Emma! What are you doing here?" she asked with asperity. Adding with a return to her usual bantering attitude towards the girl, "Why have you left the party? Has that funny friend of yours from the Workshop found himself another girl?"

To Emma's annoyance she felt the colour mounting to her cheeks. "I don't know whether he has or not," she retorted. "Actually I was looking for you to ask you not to give us any more presents." Adding with forlorn dignity, "I prefer to make my own mistakes."

Consuelo laughed with honest enjoyment. "But Geoffrey has—what do you say?—he has already had me on the carpet for that." She took Emma's arm and began to walk her back towards the hall. "And without telling you? Why is that, I wonder? Does he plan to teach you a lesson too? How very naughty of him."

Emma detached her arm from Consuelo's grip. "You are a beastly woman," she declared in a low fierce voice.

Consuelo narrowed her eyes at her. "And I can be much beastlier," she said. She walked on towards the hall.

Cedric came to look for Emma. "What's Consuelo been up to? She looks like the cat that has eaten the canary. James, on the contrary, looks ripe for murder."

"She's horrible," said Emma, with a shudder.

Cedric nodded. "Cheer up. Consuelo is always asking for trouble. She's bound to find it sooner or later. And now let us go out and see what's going on, although it's my experience that fireworks soon pall."

In the hall the men were putting on their overcoats. The women were coming down the stairs in their furs, laughing and chattering. Their feet were in fur-lined overboots. Scarves and hoods were over their heads. They shuddered in mock horror as they stepped into the cold.

In the dining room Miles appeared at Geoffrey's elbow. "Come and help me look for Harriet. William thinks he saw her on the edge of the woods."

"Right, just let me finish this." Geoffrey emptied his glass and followed his half brother. "What's the hurry?"

Miles looked round to make certain that no one else was near. "You remember I told you that Harriet had taken something of mine?"

"Yes."

"Well, it was my Browning automatic."

"Good God!" said Geoffrey blankly. "Who knows about this?"

"If you haven't heard you must be the only one in the family who hasn't," said Miles glumly. "I've been trying to catch up with her all day."

"I'm not surprised," said Geoffrey, with feeling.

They went out, walking towards the lake on the far side of which William and Ben were at work.

Miles caught Geoffrey's arm. "There she goes—into the woods as usual." They hurried forward. "Harriet!" he called. "Harriet! Wait for us."

There was no answer. No sound. Below them the rockets soared upwards and burst in a shower of gold. By its light Geoffrey, looking back, saw Emma, her face raised to the sky. By her side was the figure of Cedric, one arm thrown familiarly round her shoulders. They were both laughing.

Miles came back from the woods. He rejoined Geoffrey, who was bending forward, hands on hips, staring.

"Trouble is," Miles complained, "that Harriet must know every inch of these—" He broke off, adding hopefully, "What is it, Geoff? Can you see my wife?"

"No, I can see *mine*." Geoffrey added savagely, "She's still with that creep—and laughing." So that was why Emma had asked for a divorce. She had not only said it. She had meant it. "Miles, you'll have to find Harriet for yourself."

Miles stared after him. "Geoff, where are you going?"

Geoffrey paused. He looked back. "To get drunk," he declared.

It was now half past nine. A portrait of Her Majesty the Queen, complete with crown and sceptre, appeared in the sky. It marked the end of the display.

The guests straggled back to the house. Children were routed out of the shrubs and down from the trees. In the dining room a variety of hot savoury dishes had taken the place of the cold buffet.

Geoffrey was back in the dining room, drinking steadily. He was in process of carrying out his threat. He was soon in uproarious conversation with some of the male guests. He was interrupted by seeing Miles hovering anxiously in the doorway and staring in his direction.

He made his way across the room. "What's up now, Miles, ole boy?"

"I want you to come with me. It's important."

Geoffrey nodded, solemn as an owl. "Until this minute it was important that I got sloshed." He emptied his glass into a nearby potted plant. "Say on, Miles."

Miles hesitated. Again he glanced up and down the passage to see whether he could be overheard. There was no one near. Reassured, he said, lowering his voice, "I don't think it's been generally noticed, but now Consuelo seems to have vanished. I've hunted all through this floor. Her maid says she isn't in her bedroom. In fact, she isn't anywhere in the house."

Geoffrey considered. "In the orchid house," he suggested at last. "Several fellow enthusiasts here tonight." He was surprised that he could think so lucidly.

Miles' face cleared. "I hadn't thought of that. I'll nip out and have a look."

Left alone, Geoffrey stood, the empty glass in his hand. "Well, why not the orchid house?" he asked himself aloud.

"What is this?" James asked, coming up the passage. "An assignation?"

Geoffrey shook his head. "Miles says Consuelo is missing. Extraordinary, if true."

"It's true, all right," said James. "I have been looking for her down here. Viv has gone to see if she's upstairs."

"Any of our visitors missing? If so, she might be with them."

"Viv says not."

"And Dad?"

"Doesn't look too good." James added, "I don't want to be a scaremonger but nothing would sound more like a firework than revolver shots."

"This is the first time Miles has admitted even to himself that Harriet could be dangerous," said Geoffrey.

Said James grimly, "Before the night is out he may well have proof of it."

As they reached the hall Vivian was coming down the stairs. She saw her husband and shook her head. "Walters [this was the missing woman's personal maid] was in Consuelo's bedroom. She said she hasn't seen anything of her since she helped her dress for the party."

Grant, who had been taken into their confidence, remarked, "I haven't seen the mistress either. If she had gone out by the front door, I would have remembered."

Said James, "Consuelo could have gone by a side door. Or even through a window. Puzzle is, why should she?"

Vivian shrugged. "Well, I have Dad's heart pills and I've rung up Dr. Russel in case Dad needs him. What else can we do?"

"Grant had better telephone Rogers [the chauffeur]. And William, if he has gone to bed, must be got up again," James declared. "He and Rogers can search the outbuildings, flower garden, and shrubbery. When the guests have gone we can start something more systematic if necessary."

"I'll just pop into the dining room and pass the word to a few old cronies that Dad isn't too well. That should clear everyone off," said Vivian briskly. She was at her best in an emergency.

There she was right. Their visitors were soon once more getting into their warm clothing. Nannies appeared from the servants' hall and removed their charges. "Good nights" were said. Messages of thanks were left for their absent hostess.

No sooner had the front door closed on the last of the guests than Theodore said, "Have any of you seen Consuelo? I'm worried by her nonappearance. It's not like her. Not like her at all."

"We're all worried about her," James admitted.

"Consuelo may have met with an accident," Vivian suggested. "Fallen somewhere and twisted an ankle."

"She may have done so," said Theodore wearily. "On the other hand Harriet may have attacked her. That fear must be at the back of all our minds."

"It isn't at the back of my mind," Miles declared sullenly. His visit to the orchid house had proved fruitless. "We all know that the doctor said Harriet wasn't violent, only suicidal."

Theodore dismissed this with a tired wave of his hand. "Harriet's doctor was at some pains to say what we wanted to hear. And to do what we wanted him to do. Otherwise he wouldn't have kept her for so long."

James nodded. "I think we must accept that as true. We can't take his word for anything. Meanwhile the search must go on. And I suggest that we three"—he indicated Miles and Geoffrey—"should go down and explore the lakeside. It would be something if our only find was Harriet, staring at the water."

"Harriet has probably been in bed for hours," said Miles. "Now I think of it I remember that she didn't really like fireworks."

Vivian gave him a sharp glance. "Nonsense, Miles. We all know that she adored them." She sighed for the carefree and lovely girl Harriet had once been.

There was a momentary silence. No one was tactless enough to point out that Emma too was missing.

The three brothers set out. There was a feeling of unreality about their mission. That they would find Consuelo shot or even Harriet drowned seemed beyond the realm of possibility. They were soon involved in their own thoughts.

James was thinking of his cousin Philip. Was Vivian right, he wondered uneasily? Did Dad propose to reward him handsomely, in his will, for the twenty years he had spent as errand boy? He hoped not.

Miles was wondering about Harriet. He knew that he was not a man of decision like his father or his brother James. He asked himself uneasily whether the whole idea of bringing her back to Ilverstoke might not have been a ghastly mistake. Suppose he had done the wrong thing after all? He stumbled over a low bush and swore under his breath.

Geoffrey was thinking in a bemused way about Emma. The cold night air had dissipated much of the effect the drink had had on him. His jealousy remained unchanged.

Where were Cedric and Emma? Were they alone together at the Workshop? They certainly hadn't gone back to the party when the firework display had ended. But why get upset? Cedric, Geoffrey told himself, was welcome to Emma. What he objected to was being made a laughing-stock. He ground his teeth at the thought.

They came to the lakeside. The earlier clouds had drifted away. A full moon was reflected in the still water. Seen like this it appeared cold, remote, even sinister. Miles thought of his wife and shivered.

James clapped him on the shoulder. "Stop worrying, old chap. Tomorrow we can plan something different for Harriet. And if it *is* too late and she is in the lake, would it be so much a tragedy?"

"It would be to me," Miles answered. "I'd know I'd sent her there."

Said Geoffrey irritably, "If you two have finished your maundering, perhaps we can get on with our search for Consuelo."

James was unperturbed. "You look to me to be slightly sloshed, young Geoffrey," he said. "Apart from that, you're quite right. You go one way round the lake. Miles and I will go the other." He waited a moment, then called after the disappearing figure, "Mind you don't fall in. You'll come out of the water cold sober. Always a depressing change."

Several rude answers passed through Geoffrey's mind. It did not seem worth making them, for suddenly he had been engulfed in misery. Obviously, when they had married Emma had been too young to know her own mind, and now he had lost her.

He paused to watch where the water eddied. He knew this movement had its origin in the underground stream which ran into the lake just here. On the other hand, tonight it might be caused by some large submerged object. He looked about for a long bit of wood. He found a dead branch and poked about with it in the water.

Satisfied that neither Consuelo nor Harriet was there, he walked on, carrying the branch like a staff.

A shout reached him from the far end of the lake. Something—or someone—had been found. Geoffrey broke into a run.

His two half brothers stood very still, close to the edge of the lake. They were staring down into the still water. And, half in, half out, Consuelo Buckler stared back out of unseeing eyes.

Chapter Three

Septimus Finch was having a last drink in the bar of the small hotel where he was staying when there came a telephone call from the police station.

"This is Sergeant Scott, sir," a voice said. "We're sending a car for you. There's been a murder at Westlea Park. A Mrs. Theodore Buckler has been shot."

Shot? Then was it a pistol that Harriet had stolen from her sleeping husband? "And Superintendent Bodkin?"

"At a West End theatre with Mrs. Bodkin. He is on his way back. He asks you to carry on until he can join you."

"Right. I want Sergeant Hollis. If he's not at the station, send a car for him."

"Sergeant Hollis?" the voice sounded surprised, incredulous.

"That's what I said." Finch hung up.

When the police car arrived Hollis sprang briskly from the seat beside the driver. He looked a different man, calm, efficient, even confident. He opened the door for Finch, who got into the back and motioned Hollis to join him. "Mrs. Theodore Buckler?" he said. "That's the old man's third wife, isn't it?"

"That's right, sir, Consuelo Buckler."

"Any obvious motive?"

"Not unless it's blown up during the past few days. Mr. Grant hasn't been to the pub lately. I imagine he's been too busy. That has happened before. As for Mrs. Buckler, she was anything but popular with the two elder sons. She's managed to make a lot of trouble one way or another. Telling tales of James Buckler to his wife and of Miles to his father. Then there's Harriet Buckler. Her mother-in-law couldn't stand seeing her about and never missed an opportunity to say something unkind about her."

As he did not pursue the subject, Hollis pulled out his wallet. He took from it a plain postcard on which had been pasted the *In Memoriam* to the Frenchman.

Rather diffidently he passed it to Finch. "That came to me through the post, anonymously, sir," he said. "It's cut from the local weekly paper."

Finch read it. "With malice aforethought," he murmured. "Whoever he is, he doesn't give up."

The car swept in through the gateway of Westlea Park. The uniformed constable on duty saluted. The car drew up on a wide gravel sweep in front of a handsome pillared portico which extended the full height of the house.

In the distance, down by the lake, a light moved about. Finch regarded it with interest. "Better go down there first," he said. "Hollis, you lead the way."

The man with the torch was Detective Sergeant Topham. He was a sharp-featured man with red hair and a skin blotched with freckles. With him was P. C. Fellows. Their patrol car had been in the vicinity of the Park when the first call had gone out.

"Evening, sir," said Topham, who had looked startled on recognising Hollis. "There's not much to see here. Disappointing, too, not having the body."

Finch glanced at him, surprised. "No body? What's happened to it?"

"It seems it was found by Mr. Theodore's three sons. Lying, so they said, half in, half out of the water. They said they didn't like to leave it there, so now it's back at the house."

"Anything left behind?"

"I found two cartridge cases"—Topham held them out—"and this thread, seemingly from the blue cloak Mrs. Miles was said to have been wearing. It was found caught on a bush at the scene of the shooting."

Topham, Finch saw, was a credit hogger. He disliked the breed. "Found by the constable?" he asked blandly, and got a reluctant "Yes, sir" in reply.

"Where were the fireworks sent up from?"

"From the flat space below the white summerhouse, sir," Topham answered. "William Bolt, the head gardener, and his grandson, Ben, did the actual work. They're waiting in case you want to question them."

A thin elderly morose-looking man came forward. A gangling youth followed him. In answer to Finch's enquiries William said that he had not seen Mrs. Theodore at any time that evening. He had been astonished to learn that she had been out, since she was a lady who mistrusted the night air. Here Finch remarked that it sounded as if she had had something there, and William described how he had seen Mrs. Miles soon after the firework display had begun, standing by the gazebo, watching the rockets go up.

William's grandson, Ben, claimed to have heard several shots—he didn't know how many. At the time he had thought that one of the young gentlemen had brought some firecrackers with him and was letting them off. This had happened before. The sound had seemed to come from the far end of the lake on the opposite side to where Ben had then been standing. He put the time roughly at nine o'clock or a little before, since half the fireworks had been set off.

Finch thanked the Bolts for their help. Then told

Topham to show him the place where the body had
been found.

"This way, sir." Topham's voice dropped as he added,
"I understand that William Bolt has been with the
family as head gardener for over twenty years. It's my
belief he'll remember only what the Bucklers want him
to remember. He's a widower and lives in a cottage
high up on the ridge, looking towards the common. He
has a family, but none of them wanted to be gardeners.
You can't blame them. The old man is quite feudal in
his outlook. Even his grandson, Ben, wouldn't work
here. He's employed as a mechanic in one of the
garages in Ilverstoke."

By now they had reached the far end of the lake.
Topham indicated a bushy evergreen.

"Makes it nice and private on the other side," he
remarked. "Whoever got Mrs. Buckler there meant
business." The three men followed him to the lakeside.
"You can see where the body was taken out and that's
pretty well all you can see. We may do better when we
have some flares, but I doubt it."

Finch looked sadly at the trampled ground. "A herd
of buffalo could scarcely have been more successful in
churning up the water's edge."

"That's right, sir," Topham agreed. He added briskly,
"As for the actual murder, there's no sign of a struggle.
No broken twigs. No flattened grass."

"Just a nice private spot," Finch murmured in a
pained voice. "A fat conifer to make a screen and the
victim standing with her back to the lake, all ready to
fall into the water when shot. Most convenient."

Leaving Topham and his silent companion, the police
constable behind, Finch and Hollis retraced their steps
to the house, the former reflecting that Topham might
be a smart police officer but that he talked too much.
He hoped that Hollis was not going to err in the other
direction.

The front door of Westlea Park was opened by Grant,
the butler. He was an old man and looked frail and
shaken. "Good evening, sir. Good evening, Sergeant.

The family are waiting for you in the library, but first Dr. Russel would like a word."

The doctor was a short, dapper, self-important figure. He appeared from the direction of the inner hall, struggling into his overcoat as he came. He introduced himself to Finch. "Just want to warn you before I go. I have stimulated Mr. Theodore's heart so that he can talk to you. I would have preferred that he put no further strain on that defective organ. So be careful, please. V-ery careful!" With a light step he tripped across the floor, passed out of the house, and drove away in his car.

In the inner hall the two detectives paused to give Grant their hats and overcoats. The library door was not quite closed. A loud, mulish voice which Finch recognised came from beyond it.

"If anyone says that, I shall deny it."

"Come, Miles," said a tired but authoritative elderly voice, "what would be the sense of doing that?"

"You're all bent on getting rid of Harriet. I can see that." It was Miles speaking again.

A woman laughed, a short shrewish sound. "If you think I am going to risk being suspected so that your crazy wife can stay among us, you're very much mistaken."

"Let us agree to leave it to the police," said a smooth voice. James Buckler's? Finch wondered.

Grant threw wide the library door. "Detective Chief Inspector Finch and Detective Sergeant Hollis," he announced.

Miles looked at Finch glumly. "I thought it might be you."

"You are welcome, Chief Inspector. You too, Sergeant. I am pleased to see you although I had expected Superintendent Bodkin," said Theodore Buckler. His eyes were very keen and watchful, staring out of an alarmingly pallid face.

"He will be here as soon as he can," Finch answered in his soft voice. "Unfortunately he had taken Mrs. Bodkin to see a play in the West End."

Theodore smiled without humour. "I suppose I can

scarcely expect tragedy to occur only at a time convenient to myself."

By now Finch had taken in and identified most of the group. They all had the same look, stunned, appalled. They were, he thought, like crabs suddenly deprived of the protective shell of wealth and importance.

A girl, with the figure of a slim boy, was standing just inside the door. She looked pale, forlorn. Her eyes, Finch saw, were frightened.

Beside her stood a small man, brown-haired and brown-eyed. He looked unbecomingly cheerful and very much at his ease.

Theodore, in his introductions, had reached Emma at last. "That is my youngest daughter-in-law, Emma. She is Geoffrey's wife. With her is a friend of the family, Cedric Carter, who is a tenant of mine since he rents a stone building that stands in the woods."

"You live there?" Finch asked.

"Do you mind?" Cedric was offended. "I have a pad in West Ilverstoke."

"There is, it appears, a lot of money to be made from Mr. Carter's curious products." It was Vivian Buckler who spoke. Finch recognised that it was her waspish voice that he had heard refusing to be sacrificed for her sister-in-law.

Cedric smiled at Vivian. "You've said it. A sick industry for a sick society."

"I wish we could pursue the subject further," said Theodore wearily, "but I fear that it would be of little interest to the Chief Inspector."

"You go right ahead," Cedric told Finch. "Don't mind me."

"I understand that Mrs. Buckler's dead body was found at the far end of the lake," said Finch. "Had she any reason for going there?"

"None at all," said Theodore, "but then neither had she any reason not to go."

"And when Mrs. Buckler's body was found, it was carried back to this house?"

"At the time, it seemed unthinkable that we should

leave her there," said James in his smooth voice. "Still more unthinkable that we should have replaced her in the water. Wouldn't you agree?"

"How was Mrs. Buckler lying?" Finch asked.

"On her back. Only her head and shoulders were under water," James answered.

"We didn't realise that her death was anything but an accident," Miles declared sulkily. "Not, that is, until we'd got her out. Then we noticed that there was blood on her clothes."

"I understand that there was a party here," said Finch.

"Yes, a Guy Fawkes party. It has been held every year since my youngest son was eight. A preliminary to my own birthday, which, God help me, is tomorrow." Theodore looked ghastly for a moment. Beads of sweat broke out on his forehead but he refused his family's help and Finch's own suggestion that someone else should answer the questions.

After a moment Theodore went on. "As to who shot my wife, there are, I fancy, two possibilities. One that she was killed by some trigger-happy hoodlum, high on drink or drugs. Someone who gate-crashed the party and resented being ordered off."

"And the other possibility?" Finch asked, noting with relief that Theodore was not going to die. At least, not there and then.

Theodore sighed. "It is a probability rather than a possibility, I fear. It is only too likely that my wife was shot by Harriet, Miles' wife. She only recently came out of a mental home." He went on to speak of the accident and the loss of his grandson.

"At first it seemed moderately successful having her here, although it is true that she did not recognise Miles. Did not appear to remember her child. Evinced no surprise at finding herself living in the Lodge rather than in her old home, The Elms, which had been burnt down accidentally while she was still in the Ilverstoke District Hospital."

"Does she recognise any members of the family?"

"Not in any meaningful way," Theodore answered. "I
visited her occasionally at the mental home but visitors
weren't encouraged. The doctor felt that they only
confused my daughter-in-law."

"Was there any particular reason why Mrs. Miles
should have shot your wife?"

"Unfortunately there was. My wife was a very practical woman. She believed that if only Harriet would
accept the fact of her own guilt she would be well on
the way to being cured. Unfortunately it didn't work
out like that. Consuelo did her best to explain her
theory but the only result was to make Harriet hysterical. And in that hysteria she hated my wife. Last night
she took her husband's keys, unlocked the drawer
where he kept his automatic pistol and removed it."

"And that was what you were trying to retrieve when
we first met?" Finch asked Miles.

"Yes. I never dreamt that Harriet could hide herself
away so completely."

"Your wife knew where the gun was kept?"

"Harriet was in the room yesterday when I was
looking for an old address book," Miles answered sulkily. "I suppose she *could* have seen the automatic."

"What make was it?" Finch was thinking of the
cartridge cases.

"A Browning .32," Miles answered. "I bought it when
my wife proved such a night bird. I didn't really fancy
the front and back doors being left open for anyone to
walk in."

"And the statuette you told me about?"

"My wife took that several days ago."

Finch turned to Theodore Buckler. "When did this
confrontation between your wife and Mrs. Miles take
place?"

It was Miles who answered. "It was last Friday.
Harriet's not been herself since," he answered gloomily. "She hasn't spoken to anyone but Emma. And even
then her conversation could hardly be considered normal. She spoke of hearing voices. Said that when they
became clear she would know what to do."

"Which was to shoot her mother-in-law?"

"Which was to destroy herself," said Miles, staring around defiantly.

"Miles," said Vivian, in a voice of barely controlled irritation, "Harriet stole your gun. She must have intended to use it."

"How did your wife take the miscarriage of her plan?" Finch asked Theodore.

"Very badly. She declared that Harriet was hopelessly deranged and should be sent away. This morning she had another idea. She wanted The Elms rebuilt with a high wall enclosing it, so that Harriet could not get out."

"Did your daughter-in-law know of these plans?"

"She must have done. She was in and out of this room at all hours of the day. And I could not help noticing how her whole body stiffened when she saw my wife."

"Had your wife any reason to dislike Mrs. Miles?"

Theodore sighed. "None—beyond the fact that Harriet, sitting slumped down in her black frock, was a melancholy sight. It was one that irritated Consuelo almost beyond bearing."

"Your daughter-in-law is schizophrenic?"

Theodore frowned. "Certainly not." His face cleared. "Ah, I see what you are driving at. My daughter-in-law's protracted stay in a mental home? It was a friendly arrangement arrived at with the consent of all parties. When the mental home changed hands recently, it seemed a good opportunity to have Harriet back."

"Where is she now?"

"That is the trouble, we none of us know. During the early part of the firework display she was seen standing at the edge of the woods."

"Harriet's probably in the lake by now," said Miles bitterly. "Or she soon will be, if the police are going to hound her about."

"There will be no question of hounding your wife, but obviously she must be found," Finch told Miles. "A watch can be kept on the lake and any other local stretch of water so that she cannot drown herself." He added, "I suppose there is no possibility that Mrs. Miles might be at the Lodge?"

Miles shook his head. "I went down to see, not a quarter of an hour ago." He laughed, a jarring laugh. "It was a forlorn hope anyway. As I said, Harriet has never taken to the Lodge. She has preferred to wander about as if she were homeless."

"Has anyone else been out of doors since Mrs. Buckler's body was brought back to the house?" Finch asked.

"I have," said Geoffrey.

"For what purpose?"

"To get a breath of fresh air."

"I expect he was looking for me," said Emma sadly.

"And where were you?"

"Drinking at the Green Man with Cedric," Emma answered, as if determined to confess to the full range of her misdoings.

Theodore smiled at her. "A good thing, too," he declared. "I'm only sorry that, at your age, you have had to be involved at all."

"I'm not all that young," Emma protested.

Finch said, "I don't think that there is anything more for me to ask offhand." This was not strictly true but he did not want to be held responsible for Theodore Buckler's demise. "But there is one thing you can all do to help. If you would write down where you went in the garden. The name of anyone you spoke to during the course of the evening and when you last saw Mrs. Buckler. That way I can get some picture of the evening's events." He hesitated. "There is a warning I think I should give you. Perhaps I exaggerate. Even so, I think it must be said."

"Warn us of what?" James asked sharply.

"That Harriet Buckler, who this morning was a danger only to herself, may now be a danger to anyone she meets." And for a moment something of Finch's own anxiety transferred itself to his listeners.

Theodore broke the silence. "I can't believe that."

And then more positively, "I know Harriet. The idea is preposterous."

"Besides, we have all done our best for her since her return," said Vivian anxiously. "She has no reason to hate any of us."

Finch turned to her. "Believe me, if I am right, she will need no reason."

He left Hollis behind to keep an eye on the family. He thought that already they were recovering from the first shock. He did not want them getting together to decide what and how much to tell.

"And now if I could be shown Mrs. Buckler's bedroom," said Finch.

Theodore nodded. "James, ring the bell." When the butler appeared, his employer said, "Grant, show the Chief Inspector to my wife's bedroom. Tell him anything he may wish to know." He sank back in his chair, eyes closed, and again the perspiration was breaking out on his pallid countenance.

The bedroom was a beautiful room decorated in powder blue, grey and white. On the bed its late owner lay peacefully between the embroidered sheets.

The police surgeon came out of the adjoining bathroom, drying his hands on a fine white towel. Finch introduced himself.

"Delighted! My name is Barnet." He nodded towards the bed. "It's not often one is offered such a refined cadaver. Her maid, woman of the name of Walters, had undressed her mistress and was quite horrified when I insisted that her clothes were to be left in their present state." He laughed robustly. "I was too late to prevent her tidying up the corpse. I was determined she shouldn't do the same with its garments."

In life the third Mrs. Buckler had been a plump well-nourished and well-preserved woman of undeniable good looks, some five foot three inches high. She was wearing an elaborately trimmed nightdress. Her long, abundant dark hair had been plaited and tied with a pink ribbon. Her hands were small with pointed fingers and pale-pink painted nails. They lay crossed upon her breast.

"I understand she was found with her head under water," Barnet remarked. "Without a P.M. it's not possible to tell whether she died of gunshot wounds or drowning. Probably the latter. As you know, a gun, inexpertly fired, is not the most lethal of weapons. Three parts of the would-be suicides shooting themselves wake up in hospital and not, as they had expected, in the next world."

"And the bullets? Are they still in the body?"

"They are not. Two shots were fired right through the abdomen, the victim standing some eighteen inches from the gun. The bullets went right through her. The entry wounds, as one would expect under the circumstances, are larger than those of exit. Her outer garment shows signs of scorching. It's soiled too, with particles of partly burnt powder."

"So no particular marksmanship was needed?"

"None at all. I would imagine that Mrs. Buckler was standing facing someone when that someone produced the gun, stepped forward and fired. At that distance they couldn't miss."

Finch thanked the police surgeon. When he had gone the Yard man examined the dead woman's stomach wounds and the clothes she had been wearing. Then he wandered about staring at this and that. He made no secret of the fact that he liked to do his own poking about. He liked people. He liked their houses. He was endlessly curious—and usually it paid off.

The door opened. Superintendent Bodkin came in. He fixed Finch with a sardonic eye. "I suppose now you look on yourself as heaven's gift to this division?"

Finch shook his head. "Quite the contrary," he said blandly.

Bodkin gave a bark of amusement. "Confound your impudence. Well, at least it will be a lesson to my officers to drive more carefully in future. They'll be mad as all hell not to be working on this case." He added, with a glance about him, "How are things going?"

Finch told him. "I haven't instituted any search for Harriet Buckler," he ended. "Nor have I had a chance to interview the Geoffrey Bucklers' daily maid."

Bodkin nodded. "I'll get the search going. The daily, of course, will have to be interviewed tomorrow. I take it you'll be turning this room over?"

"Yes, sir—and any other room the late Consuelo Buckler used."

The Superintendent looked at him sharply. "I heard you'd asked for Hollis. Why?"

"I asked for him because he knows more about the Buckler family than anyone—except the Bucklers themselves."

Bodkin looked surprised. "Hollis does?"

"He has an interest in the family," said Finch dryly. "He is still convinced that he saw Justin Besson that Easter Monday. He believes that the Frenchman came here and that here the trail ended."

"The devil he does!" Bodkin considered. "Do *you* think Hollis saw this man?"

Said Finch in his gently drawling voice, "I think that someone don't like Sergeant Hollis."

The Superintendent looked at Finch searchingly. "That never occurred to me," he said slowly.

The two men went on to discuss the murder and what more could usefully be done that night. Then Finch asked how Theodore Buckler had come to know the Superintendent.

Bodkin gave an interesting answer—interesting, that is, to Finch. He said that a couple of months after Mr. Buckler had returned from his trip round the world, he had rung the police station to report that during his absence a valuable antique had been stolen. He had not disclosed its nature. Since Theodore Buckler was an important man, Bodkin had gone round to Westlea Park himself, only to learn that the missing valuable had been found. It had never been lost, only moved to a place of safety.

Hollis came into the room, walking briskly, his expression alert. He saw Bodkin and something of the old hopeless look returned. "Here are the papers you wanted, sir," he said stiffly, holding them out to Finch.

"I asked the family to write down the name of anyone they spoke to this evening and when it was they last saw Mrs. Theodore Buckler," Finch told Bodkin. He was glancing rapidly through the papers as he spoke. "Good man, Hollis! I see you got the names of tonight's guests too."

"Yes, sir. Mrs. James Buckler had a copy."

The Superintendent held out his hand. "I'll take the list of guests. First thing tomorrow my men will call on each and every one. Children are pretty sharp. I'll be surprised if no one saw Harriet Buckler or her mother-in-law." He put it into his pocket. "Now, is there anything further?"

"It might be as well to have this house watched. From what was said downstairs I had the impression that, if Harriet Buckler goes to anyone, it will be to her father-in-law."

Bodkin smiled sourly. "With the men at my disposal I couldn't mount an adequate watch on the Post Office Tower, but I'll do what I can. A nut case with a gun! I don't like it." He added, "Keep in touch and I'll do the same." He nodded to Finch, gave Hollis a hard, calculating stare, then left the room.

Finch and his sergeant began their search. The photographers arrived. They photographed the dead woman and her wounds. For good measure the fingerprint men got busy in the room in case any unauthorised person had been there that evening.

Finch rang for Grant. He asked him whether the late Mrs. Buckler had had any other room for her sole use. The butler took them down to the parlour.

Finch settled down to examine the contents of the desk. He found nothing that might have had a bearing on its owner's death. He did get an insight into one side of the dead woman's character. She had kept her accounts with computer-like accuracy. Every detail of her household expenditure was recorded, as were her investments, her allowance from her husband, and her own private income, which had been considerable.

Finch got to his feet. "Lots of jolly money and a small notebook in which Mrs. Buckler put down minor expenditures. There are several sums paid to D. Ten pounds only this morning."

"That might be Dora Short, the daily at the Small House."

"Hm! A bit odd that Mrs. Buckler should have been paying someone else's maid."

"Yes, sir," Hollis agreed. "Perhaps the girl was paid to keep an eye on the Geoffrey Bucklers. From what Mr. Grant has said at various times, nothing seems to have been too petty for Mrs. Theodore."

Finch sat down and pulled from his pocket the papers Hollis had given him earlier. He began to go through them.

"Here's something else odd," he remarked. "Young Emma writes that she last saw Mrs. Buckler just before the start of the fireworks. That would have been about eight-thirty. Consuelo was coming out of the parlour looking delighted with herself, which, Emma adds, was more than could be said for James."

"Wonder what she meant by that?" said Hollis, stopping his search.

Finch glanced at his wrist watch. "Half past one. A bit late to call at the Small House and find out."

Hollis popped his head between the heavy silk curtains and looked into the night. "There's a light still on downstairs," he announced.

"Then we'll go round there as soon as we've finished here." Again Finch rang the bell. When Grant appeared with a celerity that suggested that he had not been far away, Finch asked to speak to Miss Walters, the dead woman's personal maid.

"I regret, sir, that that will not be possible. Miss Walters was inclined to be hysterical after laying out Mrs. Theodore. Dr. Russel had to give her a sedative.

One of the housemaids sat with her until she had gone off."

When Grant had retired, Finch and his sergeant prepared to leave the house. Hollis would have liked to have looked for the ivory "Annunciation" but he did not dare to suggest it. It would have been chancing his luck too far.

A single uniformed constable stood in the vast hall. Finch saw him with some dismay. "Are you the only one on duty?"

"In the house—yes, sir. There are two men outside."

"Dear God!" said Finch, in pious horror at this paucity. And then, "How do you feel?"

The young man smiled wryly. "Inadequate, sir."

"And so you well might. Still, stick at it."

As soon as the library door had closed behind the departing Sergeant Hollis, Emma ran to Theodore.

"Dad, I'm so sorry. It seems so—so unfeeling of me to have been drinking in the Green Man while you were in such trouble."

"Nonsense, my dear." Theodore took her hand and patted it. "It simply means that there is one less person for the Chief Inspector to suspect."

"A subtle face, I thought it," said James musingly, "and vaguely familiar."

"You were lucky there—or should it be unlucky?" said Cedric, with the obvious enjoyment of the bearer of bad news. "The Chief Inspector is one of the best known of Scotland Yard's Murder Squad." He looked at Emma. "See you tomorrow?"

Emma glanced at her husband. Met only a furious regard. "I'll be there," she told Cedric mournfully.

"Good." His smile broadened as his gaze swept the family group. "At least I'll be leaving you in expert hands." He left the room.

"I think we'll be off too, Dad," said Geoffrey. "And I hope you're going to bed now."

When they had left, Theodore passed his hand over his face in a weary gesture. In spite of Dr. Russel's ministrations he felt an ominous tightness across his chest. "What an unpleasant young man he has turned out to be! So—malicious," he said, referring to Cedric. "And yet it is a good thing that Emma should go to the Workshop. I don't believe for a moment that Harriet is dangerous and she may well go there, looking for company."

"Harriet is more likely to come looking for you, Dad," said James.

Theodore nodded. "I think so too, but I was careful not to mention the possibility in front of the police. I intend to leave one of these french windows unlatched."

"You may get a burglar," Miles warned.

Vivian shivered. "Better a burglar than a madwoman," she said.

Finch and his sergeant were walking towards the Small House. "Tell me the geography of the place," said Finch.

"Well, sir, there are four houses on the estate, not counting Westlea Park itself and the Lodge. All of them are near the perimeter so as to get easy access to the road. First there is the Small House on this side of the ridge. Then, actually in the woods, is what is left of The Elms, where Miles Buckler, his wife and their small son used to live. The drive gates are kept padlocked but there is a small gate giving onto Grove Drive. This is still in use."

"I've seen The Elms from the road, or what's left of it. What else?"

"There is William Bolt's cottage. It looks over the common and has a large carpenter's shop built onto it. Lastly there is what is now known as the Workshop. That is right in the woods but on the far side of the ridge. There's no road to it. Just a rough track. Cedric Carter rents the place, as Mr. Buckler said."

Finch cast an amused glance at his sergeant. "Do I detect a certain reserve in your voice when you mention Carter?"

"Well, sir, I must admit he's not my favourite per-

son," Hollis answered. "His *pièce de résistance* is a
life-size papier-mâché effigy of the Frenchman, Besson."

"You've seen it?"

"Yes, sir. It was late one evening last June. There was
a party on at a house where the front door opened right
onto the pavement and there he was, a thin old man in
old-fashioned shabby clothes, a canvas shoulder bag, a
faded plum-coloured beret on his head and a grizzled
goatee beard on his chin."

"It matched the official description?"

"Yes, sir."

"Now that is interesting. But about the fire at The
Elms. How did it happen and how destructive was it?"

"There was never any dispute about the cause. It
seems that Miles Buckler had idolised his small son.
After his death he took to spending his time in the boy's
nursery on the first floor. On the day of the fair the two
servants had been given the day off—a well-established
custom. In the evening James Buckler arrived, for they
are a close-knit family. The two brothers had a meal.
Then, about nine o'clock, they left the house together
on one of the long walks Miles had got into the habit of
taking after dark, in the hope that it would make him
sleep.

"Later Miles agreed that he must have left a portable
electric fire on in the nursery. The wind was rising and
the window was open. The curtains blew out and into
the fire. They caught alight. The day's newspapers lying
nearby caught too. Soon the room and then the house
were ablaze. A passing motorist saw the glow and gave
the alarm. The firemen were on the scene of the fire in
a few minutes, but already there was little left to be
saved. The flames were leaping through the roof and
shortly afterwards it fell in, taking with it the first,
second, and ground floor, most of which fell into the
cellars, blocking them up except for one corner. There
remains a bit of the angle of two walls, the servants'
staircase and some of the floor above. What's left is safe

enough if you're careful. Theodore Buckler saw to it that everything that might come down was taken down."

"Everything was covered by the insurance?"

"Yes, sir."

"What was Miles' financial position at that time?"

"It so happened that he was solvent. No bills overdue. No gambling debts, which usually means that his father has just paid them."

"So—if we think there was something too convenient in the burning of The Elms, we are going against the weight of the evidence?"

"That's right, sir," Hollis agreed cheerfully.

"And the James Bucklers? Where do they live?"

"At one time they lived in one of the houses on the other side of the road. Then, about four years ago, Mr. James built himself a great big house on the far side of the common. He called it The Grange. Very modern it is. Expensive-looking too. He sold the old house. Now it's up for sale again."

"Been a bit of a nuisance to you, I dare say? An empty house always is."

"That's right, sir. The owner of one of the flats in the adjoining property is always phoning us. Hippies in the garden. People stealing plants. Not long ago it was a light in the house. We send round but it does no good. The intruders make off as soon as they see us."

Finch nodded. "Aggravating! Yes, I can see that." He paused. "About Mr. Theodore Buckler and his eldest son? Any rivalry there?"

"They don't get on too well. When Mr. Theodore was away Mr. James got used to being the boss. Even made arrangements to build, up beyond the ridge there. It's all woods now. Cleared, it would have represented a pretty profitable project."

"And that came to nothing?"

"Worse than that. Mr. Theodore found out and was furious. Threatened that if ever he found Mr. James resurrecting that project he would regret it. The quarrel died down but it left some bitterness behind. It also turned the family against Consuelo, who had done her best to keep the pot boiling. It didn't do Mr. Theodore's heart any good either. He was well enough when he got back but his health has deteriorated steadily ever since. I suppose he shouldn't have married again." Hollis broke off, wondering whether he had spoken too freely.

Finch was thinking that Hollis could talk when asked to do so. When not so asked, he remained silent. Could anything be better? He said aloud, "Have you ever visited the ruins?"

"Yes, sir, Last August, when the grounds and a couple of reception rooms were open to the public in aid of a local charity."

"Find anything of interest?"

"There was a corner of the cellar still clear. It had an upturned box there as if someone were in the habit of sitting there. Mrs. Miles, I imagine."

They were now in sight of the Small House, its white walls standing out against the dark trees. Looking in at the window, Finch saw Geoffrey Buckler sitting at a desk, a pile of papers before him. He was not working. He just sat there, glum, pale-faced, staring unseeingly before him.

Hollis put his finger on the bell push.

The sound roused Geoffrey from his unhappy preoccupation. He got to his feet with an air of great weariness that sat oddly on his youthful figure. A moment later he opened the front door.

"I'm sorry to disturb you so late," said Finch, "but I'd like a word with your wife, if she is still up. I am interested in something she wrote about the last time she saw Mrs. Buckler."

"Emma wrote something about Consuelo? Oh, you mean those wretched little summaries we all contributed. Come in while I give her a call."

Leaving the two detectives in the hall, he mounted the stairs. They heard a door open—and then another.

"Emma! Emma! Where are you?"

Geoffrey descended the stairs a great deal quicker than he had gone up. He looked disturbed. "My wife

said she was going to bed but she's nowhere upstairs.
One of her suitcases is partly unpacked too."

"Mrs. Buckler was planning to go away?"

"Not in the sense you mean. We had a row. She
packed, ready to leave as soon as my father's birthday
was over."

"What was the nature of the quarrel?"

Geoffrey answered readily enough although fleetingly,
a wary look had shown in his glance. "I was jealous of
Cedric Carter. Emma and I had a few words and in no
time it had become a furious row."

Finch nodded as if accepting this. "And now? Where
do you think she has gone?"

Geoffrey looked at Finch. There was no doubt of his
uneasiness. "I think she must be looking for Harriet.
Emma got on very well with her. Well—not that perhaps, but better than anyone else."

Finch looked at him. "Since that may not count for
much under the circumstances, you had better think
where your wife may have gone."

The furious colour ran up into Geoffrey's face. "Damn
it, I know where she's gone. To the house Harriet used
to live in. Emma often found her there searching for
Bunny—the little boy who died."

Finch was conscious of a sudden chill. "Then we'd
better get there as quickly as possible."

Chapter Four

Emma was seated on her single bed in the smallest of the guest rooms. She was thinking of Harriet. She supposed that the voices had become articulate at last. That the shooting of Consuelo had been the result.

She felt a deep sympathy for her sister-in-law. If there were a real victim, then it was she. Emma thought of her being hunted by the police, flying in front of them through the woods, knowing nothing of the reason. Experiencing nothing but blind witless terror.

But was Harriet spending the night in the woods? Or was she sheltering, as so often before, in the gutted shell of The Elms?

Emma decided to go and see.

She opened one of the suitcases she had packed earlier that day and took out clothes more appropriate to the occasion. A thick hand-knitted black sweater, denim trousers, the legs to be pushed into rubber boots, and a black crocheted cap pulled over her ears

and down to her eyebrows. It was practical if unglam-
ourous.

Purposely she tried not to think of Geoffrey. He had
rebuffed her attempts at a reconciliation. Except for
expressing regret that now it might be impossible for
her to get away as she had planned, he had had nothing
to say to her.

Emma opened the bedroom door and tiptoed to the
head of the stairs. The house was very silent. A streak
of light showed under the door of Geoffrey's workroom.
It was, she told herself, no more than she had expected.
It had been an unwritten law that she never disturbed
him there. In the old days—that is until this morning—
he had only gone there to work. Now he was using the
room to avoid her.

Stealing silently and sadly down the stairs, she let
herself out by the back door.

A slight breeze had sprung up, setting the clouds
scurrying across the sky. At the moment everything was
dark. It did not hamper her. The path was wide and
clear of obstacles. A box hedge showed black on one
side.

Emma, having scanned the sky with a weather eye,
decided, as she pushed her way through the hedge,
that the next day would be windy and rough. There
might even be rain. This thought seemed to make more
urgent the need to find Harriet.

She was now in what had once been the rose garden
of The Elms. It had as its centrepiece a fountain, its
bowl full of stagnant water.

The breeze dropped. Except for a thin piping of
traffic on the main road, the night was still. The cracking of a twig underfoot or the rolling of a pebble
sounded unnaturally loud.

The moon came out from behind a cloud and she
could see the giant elms from which the house had
taken its name. One of them had come down a few
weeks before. There had been talk of cutting down the
others for safety's sake but nothing had been done. The
blackened, dingy, once-yellow-brick walls of the burnt-

out building still soared crazily upwards in the ring of ancient trees.

Emma found herself moving silently and cautiously. She did not know why. Except that the scene now held a strangeness and a desolation that was absent during daylight hours.

She walked into the house where the front door should have been. Picked her way among the rotting joists and came on the entrance to the one remaining clear corner of the cellars. She bent down, peering into the darkness—"Harriet, are you there?"—and heard her voice echo in the empty foundations of the house, setting off a chain reaction of other indefinable sounds.

The opening into the cellar was through a triangular space made by three floor joists. Emma, squatting there, swung the light of her torch into every corner of the enclosure below. She saw the broken box on which Harriet would sit, perfectly still, hands folded in her lap, and an expression on her face that Emma always thought of as bewildered and lost. She saw rats scurrying away to disappear behind the pile of rotting timber and plaster which had filled up the rest of the cellar, but of Harriet herself there was no sign.

One end of the house had escaped the worst of the fire. Here was the bit of the angle of two walls mentioned by Hollis, rising up some thirty feet. Clinging to it was what had once been the servants' stairs. They led to where part of the flooring was left, supported from underneath but open to the sky.

Emma went up the steep steps keeping to the inner side, her hand on the wall, for the wooden banister had burnt down to stumps and now stuck up like blackened swollen fingers.

She counted as she climbed.

Twenty-one, twenty-two, twenty-three—she had reached the top. She stepped onto the remaining boards where the moonlight came in through an empty window frame and lay like a rug on the dusty floor.

Harriet was not here either. Disappointed, Emma turned to retrace her steps, moving cautiously yet aware of a sudden sharp desire to be gone from this rotting and derelict place.

The moon went behind a cloud. Now Emma must switch on her torch or depend on her sense of touch. Moving crabwise, hand outstretched, she began silently to count. One, two, three, four— She halted abruptly, holding her breath, her flesh creeping.

The conviction had come to her that she was no longer alone. The very air of that velvet well of darkness seemed tenanted. The night became full of tiny sounds. The house began to stir. Noises muffled and hollow broke on her ears. She had, too, the uncomfortable feeling that she was perfectly visible to the someone— or something—that lurked in the darkness below her.

Harriet? Was it Harriet? She felt no desire to call out. On the contrary, she crouched lower, pressing herself to the wall, hoping with every shuddering fibre of her being that she would not be discovered.

From somewhere in the darkness below came a rattle of small pebbles falling into the cellar. Whatever was in the house was moving about. Coming towards the stairs? A fresh spasm of terror froze her where she crouched.

The moon reappeared. By its light Emma saw the familiar figure of Harriet, Harriet in her blue cloak. Harriet, hood drawn forward, each hand thrust up the opposite sleeve for warmth.

At the same moment Emma became aware of distant but approaching footsteps hurrying along the path. Geoffrey's voice called crossly, "Emma!" There was a cracking and a swishing of the box hedge. A voice she recognised as belonging to the Chief Inspector called, "Mrs. Geoffrey! Are you there?" And still Emma did not move. She was listening intently to Harriet's footsteps becoming fainter and fainter on the night air.

As soon as they had gone completely, she hurled herself recklessly down the remaining stairs. She came scrambling and leaping through the tangle of weeds and rose briars.

"Hullo!" Emma clutched Finch by the arm, kneading

it with small frantic clutchings. "Am I glad to see you! Oh—oh, it was spooky there. Things I'd never noticed before stood out in a threatening kind of way. And things I did know had disappeared as if they were no longer there. The whole place looked different."

"Looked different?" Finch echoed. "It is different. You should have stayed at home." He could feel her slim body shivering at his side. "Night is the time for the predators."

"Owls and rats," said Emma.

"And Harriet Buckler?"

"She was there—just for a moment."

"Did you speak to her?"

"No, I didn't," Emma answered shortly.

Finch glanced at his sergeant. "Get the search party going up here," he said. "I'll pick you up later, outside the big house."

Emma glanced askance at Hollis. "You won't find her. Harriet—just melts." She giggled nervously.

Finch drew Emma's hand through his arm. "What you want is a hot drink."

"We'd better get back to the house," said Geoffrey stiffly. He had not looked at his wife. He had kept his gaze on what Finch, amused, thought of as the middle distance.

Soon Emma's hand ceased to clutch. Her breathing quieted down. "Had you any particular reason for wanting to see me?" she asked.

"You mentioned seeing Mrs. Buckler coming out of the parlour. You said she looked pleased?"

"So she did. I was bored with the party, so"—Emma cast a sidelong glance at Geoffrey, who only made a gesture of impatience—"I decided to find Consuelo and tell her to leave us alone. She does—did—interfere in everything." Emma went on to recount how she had tried to catch her husband's eye so that she could smile at him. And here she peered anxiously and surreptitiously across Finch to Geoffrey's stony profile, hoping for some return from him for this confidence, secondhand though it had been. When he took no visible notice she gave the faintest of sighs, before embarking on her story of seeing first her brother-in-law and then Consuelo. When she had ended she looked at Finch searchingly. "Why are you interested in James?"

"Not in him particularly. It is just part of the system. When the final report goes in, there will be statements on everyone."

"I don't think that's right," said Emma firmly.

"We all complain of paper work," said Finch mildly, "but it goes on just the same." Emma snorted disapprovingly through her short nose.

In the Small House all the lights were burning. They gave a welcoming air. Welcome, too, was the warmth.

Emma pulled off her cap and crouched, long-legged, before one of the radiators. "It is nice to be back," she remarked. And then, "I don't think I have ever been so pleased to see anyone as I was to see you two."

"You seem to have a hitherto unsuspected genius for frequenting undesirable localities," said Geoffrey coldly.

"I have not," Emma cried, stung by this injustice.

"You didn't consider the Green Man a rather peculiar choice when Consuelo was being murdered?"

"It would have been much more peculiar if I had refrained from going there because I suspected that she *was* going to be murdered," Emma retorted, but without much conviction.

Geoffrey shrugged. "I'll make some coffee," he said. He walked away down a passage. He closed the kitchen door behind him. They heard him faintly, banging the saucepans together.

Emma sighed and Finch said, "You didn't like your mother-in-law?"

Emma shook her head. "She was jealous of Dad's family. When she first came, and until fairly recently, she was at war with James and Miles. Lately she's been concentrating on me. This morning things came to a head." She told him of the disastrous happenings at the breakfast table. "In five years' time *I* could get a divorce but I don't want one. I like being married— particularly to Geoffrey."

Finch assured her solemnly that he felt certain that Geoffrey liked being married too—and to her. He offered, if necessary, to bring him to his senses by pretending to suspect her. This seemed to cheer her up and Finch took the opportunity to enquire why Miles Buckler had said that his wife never went near The Elms.

"Harriet didn't want him to know. She said, 'He's angry with me. I don't know why and I think he'd be angrier still if he knew I came here.'"

"Did she give any reason for going to The Elms?"

"She was trying to remember about Bunny. 'Something terrible happened here—only I can't remember.' She would say it so sadly and wonderingly that it was enough to make one want to cry. And it wasn't any use telling her that Miles wasn't angry."

"She didn't believe it?" Finch asked interestedly. "Or she didn't take it in?"

"Harriet didn't believe it. If I tried to explain how he'd changed, she would get agitated and—and more frightened."

Geoffrey returning with a loaded tray, looked at them sourly. "I thought we might go into the dining room," he said distantly.

Except where matrimony was concerned, he was, Finch reflected, a man after his own heart. On the tray were beakers of hot soup, open sandwiches, a variety of cheeses, rolls and butter. Even a dish of olives—which later on his host ate with a gloomy air.

Finch refused his offer of whisky and took the soup. "I was given a rather sketchy description of the encounter at the Lodge between Mrs. Theodore and her daughter-in-law. In view of the state of Mr. Theodore's health, I didn't like to press him for more details." He looked across the polished table top to where Geoffrey sat, a rather inscrutable look on his lantern-jawed face. "How much do you know of this?"

"About what happened? Nearly everything," Geoffrey answered. "It was last Friday afternoon. James and Miles were still in the City. My wife and I were coming back from a walk on the common. We were still quite a way from the Lodge when we heard Harriet screaming abuse. 'Liar,' she kept calling." Geoffrey grinned briefly. "Or words to that effect."

"And banging," Emma added. "We couldn't think what was happening."

"The front door is never locked now, so we had no difficulty getting in," Geoffrey went on. "We'd never seen such a sight. There are—or were—four oak chairs in the hall and she'd broken them all, battering at the door of the downstairs cloakroom behind which Consuelo had taken refuge. As we came in, Harriet was staring round for something else to use. Her eyes passed over us but I'll swear she didn't see us. She didn't hear us when we spoke either. She looked extraordinary. Like one of the Furies. She was grinding her teeth. Her dress was in shreds. Her hair had come down and was all over her face. Her eyes glittered like those of a madwoman. She had cut her hand and there was blood on her chin.

"Her eyes fell on a small, heavy oak table. She gave a sort of grunt of satisfaction, seized it and lifted it up above her head. She began to crash it against the door, and I had begun to have visions of what would happen if Consuelo, Harriet and myself were involved in a general melee, when Dad walked into the hall. He had been passing in his car when he'd heard the row Harriet was making."

"He was wonderful," said Emma. "He walked straight up to her and said, 'That will do. My poor child, you're wearing yourself out.'"

"There was a sort of ghastly pause," said Geoffrey reminiscently. "Then Harriet gave a sob, dropped the table and went to Dad, crying like a baby."

"And your stepmother?" In the light of this story Theodore Buckler's description of Harriet as hysterical hardly seemed entirely adequate, Finch reflected, grimly amused.

"Consuelo wouldn't come out of the cloakroom until Harriet was asleep in bed," said Emma. "She was all to pieces and her hair was coming down. When she caught sight of herself in a mirror she was terribly mortified."

"And Mr. Theodore?"

"He had gone back to the house in the car. And d'you know?"—Emma's eyes were round—"he never sent it back for her. That's how angry he was."

"I saw Consuelo home," said Geoffrey. "She was in no fit state to go alone."

"Geoffrey was sorry for her but I wasn't, and now she's dead." Emma added hopefully, with a sidelong glance at her husband, "It just shows one should never allow the sun to go down on one's anger."

After an empty pause, Finch asked how Harriet had been next day.

"I don't really know," said Emma, sighing. "Saturday and Sunday she wouldn't speak to anyone. I know Vivian—James's wife—tried to talk to her but I don't think Harriet made any response. It's odd really. Vivian's always trying to be friendly and yet I have a feeling she dislikes Harriet. I know she never went to see her when she was in the mental home."

"Perhaps she is trying to make up for her previous neglect," Geoffrey said coldly.

Emma looked at him with astonishment. "You've said yourself that Vivian would rather die than admit that she had been in the wrong."

Conquering a desire to laugh, Finch rose to his feet. He thanked the two young people for their help and their hospitality. They went with him to the front door.

"I suppose," said Emma, "that if Harriet had been found you would have heard?"

"Yes." Finch consulted his wrist watch. "By now, everyone has probably given up the search and gone home."

"All the police can't have gone," said Emma. "There must be someone left on guard in Consuelo's bedroom."

Finch stared across at the big house. It looked enormous, darkly outlined and somehow rather menacing. "What makes you say that?"

"Because there is a light shining between the curtains. Look! It's the two windows above and to the right of the light over the front door."

"Perhaps Dad is in there," Geoffrey suggested.

Emma shook her head. "It's not likely to be Dad. The light was on when we got back here and that's more than an hour ago."

"We'd better get over there." Finch turned to Geoffrey. "Have you a key?"

"Yes, I can let you in."

Emma clutched at Finch's arm. He thought that she had turned pale. "I'm not going to be left here. I don't mind waiting downstairs while you go up to the bedroom but I won't stay here."

"For heaven's sake, why not?" Geoffrey cried irritably.

"Because," said Emma with a shudder, "if I were alone Harriet might get in. If that happened I think I should die of horror."

"Then by all means come," said Finch. He could feel that Emma was shivering again. She cast glances to right and left as they went, as if she suspected every bush, every tree, of harbouring her sister-in-law.

A man's figure detached itself from the shadow cast by the house. It was Hollis. "Anything wrong, sir?"

"I don't know yet." Finch explained about the lights. "How many men are still about?"

"Only the two watching outside the house and P. C. Martin standing in the hall," Hollis answered.

By this time they had reached the house and Geoffrey was unlocking the front door. "There are two locks," he explained. "A mortice as well as a Chubb. At night, Grant locks them both." By the light over the front door Finch saw that he looked pale and anxious.

A single wall light burnt in the inner hall. Another shone from the first-floor landing. The uniformed figure of P. C. Martin stepped forward but Finch waved him back. "Later," he said, and went with Geoffrey up the stairs. Since no one said anything about Emma staying downstairs, she followed at a discreet distance.

Geoffrey took the wide, shallow stairs three at a time. As he threw open the bedroom door he tensed himself

as if he expected to be faced by a belligerent intruder.
He gave a cry of distress. Finch, looking over his
shoulder, stiffened involuntarily.

The body of Consuelo Buckler had been removed
from the room. It had been replaced by another. Sprawled
on the floor, motionless on the thick, grey-pile carpet
was Theodore Buckler. He was still fully clothed, except that he had exchanged his jacket for a dressing
gown. A chair lay on its side behind him and a small
low table with a broken leg lay close to his outflung
hand.

Geoffrey dropped on to his knees beside his father.
"Dad!" he called, "Dad!" while Emma crouched shivering
behind him.

Finch too had knelt beside the still figure. Now he
stood up. "It's no good," he said. "Your father has been
dead for some time." He added, to give the young man
something to do, "You had better telephone your
brothers."

Emma wiped the tears from her cheeks with the back
of her hand in a schoolboy gesture. "I'll come with you,
Geoffrey," she said.

As the door closed behind them, Finch knelt down
again. This time beside the overturned table. He stud-
ied its surface from several angles. There were faint
signs visible that someone had stood on it. Probably
"Forensic" would be able to make more of it, he
thought. He wanted the room gone over once more for
fingerprints and the house searched for Harriet. She
must be somewhere near.

He went downstairs and put all this in hand. Then he
spoke to P. C. Martin. "I expect you have heard that
Mr. Buckler, senior, is dead. It looks like heart failure.
Did you hear anything of it?"

"I heard something fall, sir," Martin answered. "A
right heavy bump from the first floor. That was at 2:14
A.M. I went upstairs and knocked, Mr. Grant having
pointed out Mr. Buckler's bedroom door earlier on.
Nothing happened so I tried the handle. The door was
locked. Then, just as I was thinking of going for help,

the gentleman opened it. I could see that under his dressing gown he was fully dressed. His face was grey and the sweat was standing out on his forehead. He said that he was sorry that he had disturbed me but that he'd knocked something off his bedside table. I asked if I should send for his doctor but he said no. That he had been a bit restless but that now he was going to bed. I heard him turn the key in the lock and I stood there for a couple of minutes, hoping he'd be all right. I suppose it was because of the thickness of the carpet that I couldn't hear him moving away."

Finch raised an eyebrow. "You expected to hear him?"

Martin was a young man and afraid of ridicule. He turned very pink. "Well, sir, I know it sounds daft but I thought, when I went downstairs, that I'd left him still there, on the other side of the door."

Finch nodded. "Interesting," he murmured. "What did you think when you first heard the thump?"

Said Martin simply, "I thought that Mr. Buckler had had a heart attack and fallen. When it actually happened I heard nothing."

The police surgeon arrived once more. The finger-print men came and half a dozen rather disgruntled plain-clothes men to search for Harriet.

Miles Buckler arrived on foot. He looked heavy-eyed. His hair was untidy and his clothes wrinkled. James followed with his wife. He was driving a handsome Bentley saloon. He looked as neat and as meticulously dressed as usual. Vivian, if composed, looked plainer than ever.

"This is terrible news but not to be wondered at," James said, wringing Geoffrey's hand and kissing Emma on the cheek. "Poor old Dad! Lucky he'd pretty well retired from the company."

Miles' face coloured. "We lose the best father in the world and all you can think of is the effect of his death on the company's shares."

"It's not *all*," James answered. "It is one aspect."

"And one that your father would have been the first to want considered," Vivian declared firmly.

Philip Wheatley came in. He expressed sorrow at his uncle's death.

Miles glared at him. "Who invited you to stick your nose in?"

"I telephoned him," said Geoffrey. He spoke not aggressively but with decision. "He's been like a fourth son to Dad for years. He had a right to know."

Miles looked astounded. "A fourth son? You must be mad."

James and his wife exchanged a quick glance. "Well, let's call it a right hand. No one could quarrel with that," said James pacifically.

"Dad certainly provided for him for long enough—if that makes him either a fourth son or a right hand," said Miles disagreeably.

Philip said nothing. His faint smile might have been painted on his face.

"Let's go into the library," Geoffrey suggested. "The place is crawling with policemen again. I can't think why."

When they got there, Miles looked round the room as if it were haunted. "Isn't there somewhere else we could go? This was Dad's room."

"And this is Dad's business," James retorted, a touch of grimness in his voice. As he spoke he was pouring out a stiff whisky for his brother.

Geoffrey launched into an account of his coming over to the house and what had been found. He had just finished when Finch and Hollis entered the room.

James was spokesman for the family. "Have you any idea what happened upstairs to give my father such a shock that he died of it? For instance the overturned chair and table?"

"Dad probably caught at the chair so that he could sit down when he first felt a heart attack coming on, but didn't quite make it," Miles suggested.

"What we're really getting at is to find out whether

Harriet could have been in the room. And if so, why?"
said James.

"That's not likely," said Geoffrey. "Harriet was the
one person who hadn't any keys."

"You forget that Harriet wouldn't have wanted them,"
said James. "Dad left one of these french windows
unlatched in case she came looking for him."

Geoffrey stared. "I didn't know that."

James nodded. "I'd forgotten. You and Emma had
already left when Dad told us." He added grimly, "Viv
didn't think much of the idea at the time. It seems she
was right."

"Viv has a way of being right," said Philip.

Finch thought that he detected a faintly derisive note
in Philip's voice. James must have heard it too, for he
glanced in surprise and some disquiet at his cousin.
Wondering where Dad's money is going, Finch thought.
He had not made any comment so far. Had simply
stood there, bland and slightly somnolent-looking. Far
more useful to let the Bucklers do the talking, he had
reflected. Now he tried the three long windows. He
found that the centre one only wanted a push to open
it.

Geoffrey said, "Then it was probably Harriet who
came in. Emma saw her tonight at The Elms."

"The Elms?" Miles echoed blankly. "But Harriet
never goes near the place."

"Yes, she does," said Emma. "I don't think she
remembers that she ever lived there or anything like
that. It's just that she has a vague idea that something
awful took place there. She wants to remember what it
was."

"I wish I'd known," said Miles bitterly, "but then I
don't seem to know anything about Harriet." His voice
rose wildly. "Perhaps she did haunt The Elms. Perhaps
she did take my automatic and shoot Consuelo. For all I
know, she may even have frightened Dad to death."

"Miles, you're putting yourself on the rack to no
purpose." James put an arm about his brother's shoul-

ders. "Come back and spend the night—what's left of it— with us."

"Or stay with us," Geoffrey offered. "Or we'll stay with you."

"That last is the better offer," said James. He smiled at his young sister-in-law, a genuine gleam of amusement in his eyes. "Emma hardly ranks as one of our more notable hostesses."

Miles gave a harsh laugh. "You're all too bloody kind. I'm walking back to the Lodge. I'm going to have a stiff drink, a hot bath and a couple of hours' sleep."

"Good idea," said Philip affably. "Well, I suppose we shall be seeing some changes here. Good night, everyone." He left an uneasy and startled silence behind him.

Finch waited until the room was empty and the sound of departing cars had faded in the distance. Then he went to speak to the fingerprint men, who were about to go off duty. Sergeant Topham, looking morose, was with them.

"That is an interesting thing, sir," said one of the men. "Since we were here last, that bedroom has had a good going-over."

"Don't tell me you found fingerprints in the late Mrs. Buckler's room?"

The man grinned. "Far from it, sir. Whoever it was was wearing gloves. He mucked up your prints and those we'd taken earlier."

Topham waited until he was alone with Finch. Then he said with barely concealed hostility, "What's this about an open library window, sir? They were all fastened at 2:10 A.M., for I tried them—"

As he spoke he saw the probable explanation. The colour rushed to his cheeks. "So when I tried those windows Harriet Buckler had just fastened them behind her." He struck a clenched fist into the palm of the other hand. "Dolt that I am! I had her trapped and never realised it."

"So it would seem," said Finch dryly.

Back at the police station Superintendent Bodkin was

in his office. In front of him on the large, flat-topped desk was a depleted plate of sandwiches, a Thermos of coffee and a litter of dirty cups.

When he saw Finch he indicated, with a table knife, the face of the electric clock, which showed the time to be 4:35 A.M. "Marvellous, isn't it? Every time I thought of going home, something new turned up. This is the third meal I've eaten here. First, everyone was searching for Harriet Buckler in the woods. Then, everyone was searching for her at The Elms. Next, Theodore's dead body was found. That wasn't murder—just natural causes. No matter. Soon everyone was back there again, looking for fingerprints and for Harriet, who is still missing."

"Wonder if we shall find her tomorrow?"

"Of course we will. And we'll begin by dragging the lake and the two ponds on the common. No point in mounting an all-out search for her if she's gone and drowned herself. I'll get a couple of police frogmen too. They can search the lakeside for Miles Buckler's Browning. Here, have some coffee." Bodkin was pawing about among the medley of used crockery. "There must be a clean cup somewhere. Ah! Here it is. Help yourself— and don't take much sugar. I'm told it creates energy and we don't want you taking off again."

Finch poured himself a cup of coffee. "And when we have Harriet, dead or alive, will that close the case?" He looked dubiously at the Superintendent. "I don't like it. True, the bare bones are straightforward enough. A is rich, spoilt and mischief-making. B is just out of a mental home. The potentially dangerous situation between them exploded last Friday. B broods. On the Monday night she steals her husband's automatic. On the following evening during a firework display B shoots A and, for good measure, leaves A with her head under water."

Bodkin's small, shrewd eyes narrowed. "Too pat? I'm inclined to agree with you."

"It's a solution I've had pressed on me several times this evening. Miles is the only one against it."

Bodkin gave his loud guffaw. "No, sir. Please, sir. It wasn't me, sir. It was Harriet." He investigated the contents of a sandwich with a disparaging eye. "Does Miles Buckler suspect that someone is trying to frame his wife?"

"Could be. He's certainly living in a state of high tension."

There was silence for a little while Finch drank some coffee and Bodkin ate another sandwich.

"How about Hollis' obsession? The chap who worked in ivory?"

"He has made a brief, indirect appearance." Finch took out his wallet. From it he produced the cutting given to him on the previous evening. "This came to Hollis anonymously through the post yesterday. A cutting from the Ilverstoke *Gazette*."

Bodkin looked at it. "So we're back with the French connection, are we?" He gave a roar of laughter. "D'you get it? That old film—*The French Connection*?"

Finch was pained. "I get it—but, if there is a connection, I can't see where Harriet comes in."

Bodkin nodded. "Is Harriet's mind capable of appreciating the advantages to be gained by shooting someone during a barrage of sounds of a somewhat similar nature? Well, is it?"

"I don't know." Finch's thoughts moved on. "This chap, Cedric Carter? Is he known to the police?"

"Not in the sense you mean. Why? You don't suspect him of being involved in the killing of Consuelo Buckler?"

"I see him as being very nicely placed to influence Harriet, who, it is generally agreed, spends most of her time in the woods. And, except for young Emma, he don't like the Bucklers."

"I see. Well, I've met Carter in the course of business. My business. Nothing official. The fact is"—Bodkin's voice grew fond—"my youngest daughter had set her heart on having one of his trendy gifts as a birthday present. And, since I was in his shop, I was interested in the setup." Absently Bodkin took another sandwich. "Cedric Carter's shop is in West Ilverstoke, where there is a large student and teen-age population. Over the shop there's a workroom where about a dozen young people are employed making papier-mâché objects. Mind you"—he wagged a finger at Finch—"Carter is smart. He not only fulfils a need, he first created it—and you can't get much smarter than that."

Finch had been trying to picture the Superintendent as an indulgent parent—or indeed as a parent at all. He found it called for too much of an effort, at least at that time of the morning. He said, "We know that Theodore Buckler left a french window open for Harriet. We don't know that it was Harriet who came in—"

"And it's quite possible"—Bodkin gave a huge yawn—"that whoever it was had nothing to do with the murder of Consuelo Buckler but was simply an opportunist taking advantage of what had happened."

"In that case I fancy Theodore Buckler would have got himself a doctor."

Bodkin did not agree. "Too far gone for that. What was it Martin said? Grey and sweating?" He was considering the last sandwich. Should he? Or should he not? "Martin's a sound-enough fellow but not imaginative."

"That's what I thought." Finch was glad to have the Superintendent in agreement with him. "'A primrose by a river's brim/a yellow primrose was to him,/And it was nothing more.'"

Bodkin took the last sandwich. "If you're thinking of getting everyone out again to look for primroses, forget it. They don't flower this time of year."

He burst into a roar of laughter, laughing until his eyes watered.

Chapter Five

The morning dawned cold and overcast. A fitful wind rippled across the still waters of the lake, bending the tall grasses and bringing down the leaves in clouds before subsiding once more. Shortly after five o'clock there had been a heavy shower of rain.

The two policemen on duty by the lake stamped their feet to restore the circulation and cursed the hours of darkness during which nothing but tedium and discomfort had been their lot.

Miles Buckler had been out too when the dark was not yet lifted. When searching was a matter of calling out, of stumbling over branches brought down by the wind and tripping over trailing briars.

Emma, standing at the open bedroom window, had heard his voice, hoarse, echoing: "Harriet! Harriet! Where are you?"

The police on duty at the lakeside heard it too, faintly at first, then louder.

The younger of them put into words what was in both their minds. "Queer, you never think of people like that having troubles. But, boy, oh boy, hasn't he got them?"

At the police station telephone calls were coming in from people who thought they had seen Harriet Buckler— at a railway station, on a bus, signing the hotel register at some South Coast resort. The telephone rang and rang. Most, if not all, of this information would prove worthless. All of it had to be followed up.

Some of the guests reported having seen the cloaked figure of Harriet in the distance when they were leaving after the Guy Fawkes party. They had waved but this had not elicited any response.

There was more trustworthy news of Consuelo's actions during the last hours of her life. A small boy, guest at the Guy Fawkes party, who had been amusing himself staring in at the many lighted windows, had seen Consuelo come out of a side door. His mother had been friendly with her so that there was no question of his having been mistaken. She had been unexpectedly angry with him: "For spying. A child of that age!" his mother had said indignantly to the plain-clothes man.

A Mrs. Parker and her husband had also seen Consuelo. They had been standing in the shadow of a beech hedge, not far from the house, when she had hurried past, going towards the far end of the lake. They had not spoken to her, partly because she had appeared to be in a great hurry, but mostly because they didn't know her well, being friends and contemporaries of the Geoffrey Bucklers.

Two schoolboys, aged twelve and eleven, had seen Harriet at the far end of the lake. She had been standing quite still, staring across the water. She had not seen them and, having heard that she was mad, they had silently withdrawn before she could do so. No, they had not seen her again. They did not think that they would recognise the exact spot where they had seen her.

Finch gazed almost fondly at these reports. "So that's it," he drawled in his soft voice. "We have a joker in the pack. The same person who searched Consuelo's bed-room must previously have lured her to the lakeside so that Harriet could shoot her."

Bodkin stared. "How d'you make that out?"

"Because," Finch answered happily, "whoever else the late Mrs. Buckler had expected to see when she went out, it would not have been Harriet."

The big gates of Westlea Park were closed against sightseers. The two uniformed constables saluted when they saw Finch. One of them opened the gates, while the other shepherded back the small crowd which had gathered.

"Everything quiet?" Finch asked.

"Yes, sir. There's been quite a bit of traffic. Caterers, florists and the like, all connected with the party. Nothing else."

Finch and Hollis walked up the path to the Lodge.

A respectable-looking woman in an overall answered their ring. This was Mrs. Partridge, who came in daily to do the housework. She was showing them into the sitting room when Miles Buckler called out to know who was there.

"Chief Inspector Finch and Sergeant Hollis," Finch answered.

They heard a chair pushed back in the dining room. Miles appeared in the doorway, a table napkin in one hand.

"No news, I suppose?"

"None." Finch was shocked at the change in Miles. His face was grey with fatigue, and he looked years older. He had cut himself shaving and a couple of scraps of plaster did nothing to improve his looks. "I won-dered whether you could think of anyone to whom your wife might have gone?"

"If I could have, I'd have been round there myself," Miles retorted. Adding, "Have some breakfast? It's a queer thing but from not being able to eat a bite, suddenly I was ravenous. Just having my third boiled egg and I've lost count of the number of pieces of toast I've eaten."

In the dining room the two detectives were greeted by Emma. She was dressed as she had been for her expedition to The Elms on the previous night. She was subdued and her eyelids were swollen with crying, but she seemed pleased to see them.

"I heard Miles calling Harriet early this morning so I got up and joined him," she said in explanation of her presence at the Lodge. "Not that we did much good."

"That's true." Miles sat down again at the table. "Harriet's got me flummoxed. Where could she have gone if she isn't in the woods?"

Emma sighed. "It is extraordinary the way she seems to have disappeared."

"Would you know if Mrs. Miles had taken any food out of the fridge?" Finch asked her husband.

Miles shook his head. "There's masses of food about. I have it sent in ready-cooked but whether any of it is gone I wouldn't know."

"When your wife first returned did you try and find out where she went at night?"

"If she slept, it was in that little gazebo above the lake," Miles answered. "And if she wasn't asleep I'd catch glimpses of her moving away from me like a—well, like a spirit, quick and silent. After the first couple of weeks I left off worrying." He added, "Of course there used to be several men who were keen on her. Philip Wheatley, for one. Yet I can't see him hiding her now. For one thing a lot of water has flowed under the bridge since then. For another he used to hang round Consuelo— even if it was at my father's bidding."

"Does Mr. Wheatley live near here?"

"Yes, in Waterloo House. It's a big place and, like most of the others in Grove Drive, it has been turned into flats. You can't miss it. It's next door to one with sale boards in the hedge. Brother James managed to get rid of that white elephant. Its present owners haven't been as lucky. It's an awkward house to convert."

"But that wouldn't be James' fault," Emma argued. "I've heard Geoffrey say it's no longer a seller's market."

"D'you think your wife still has your pistol?" Finch asked Miles.

"Never in this life. She may have cached it away somewhere, but she wouldn't be lugging it around with her."

"How familiar was she with firearms?"

Miles made a grimace. "She was a good shot," he admitted. "We both belonged to a rifle and pistol club," adding hastily, "but Harriet wouldn't remember anything of that."

"Still it was lucky Harriet didn't have your automatic last Friday when Consuelo made her so angry. She might have shot all of us," Emma commented.

"In any case that was all over before you got home, wasn't it?" Finch asked Miles.

"It was not. Harriet frightened me half out of my wits." Miles laughed shortly. "When I got home that evening—and by bad luck I was late—there were no lights on in the house. And before I could turn them on, Harriet had come gliding down the stairs." Miles glanced directly at Finch. "I don't know if you have noticed what an extraordinary walk my wife has now? Anyway there she was, in a long white nightdress, another idea of that damned mental home. She caught my hand and hissed—blow if I've ever heard anyone else do it. She hissed, 'Did you know she was responsible? Consuelo! She killed our baby.' I was—well, frankly I was scared out of my wits. I'd have given anything at that moment to have had someone else in the house with me. I put the lights on and tried to reason with her but I could see I wasn't having much effect. She just stood, stiff as a board, repeating over and over, 'She killed our baby. That's what she came round to tell me. She killed—'" Miles broke off with an embarrassed laugh. "Sorry. I seem to have caught the habit."

Emma shook her head sadly. "I should never have left her, but she did seem so soundly asleep."

"So," Finch commented thoughtfully, "your wife does remember that she had had a child."

"Of course she does. I wonder sometimes how much—" Miles broke off to continue, "Harriet had transferred her own sense of guilt to Consuelo, that's what Dr. Russel said when he got here. Anyway the fight seemed to go out of her quite suddenly. She turned round and went back to bed. She was asleep in no time."

The front-door bell rang. There was the sound of voices in the hall. Vivian Buckler came into the dining room.

She nodded to the two detectives. "Good morning— if you can call it that." She added, "As I walked over the common I saw the police dragging one of the ponds, so I take it that there is no news of Harriet?"

Miles sprang to his feet. "Damn it! That's too bad. Why didn't someone let me know? I'll have to go."

"I'll come too," said Emma, rising from her chair.

"Miles, you can't," Vivian protested. "The common is thick with people, all staring and making comments. Your appearance would cause a sensation."

"Much I care for that!" Miles nodded a general farewell. "So long!"

Vivian caught him by the arm. "But James says he must see you. There's so much to be decided. Geoffrey is already there. Philip too, in case he is needed."

Miles laughed shortly. "Tell James I'll be along later to give his decisions my blessing and, where necessary, my signature."

Vivian looked at Miles sharply. "If you don't stop worrying you'll end up as crazy as Harriet." She bit her lip. "I didn't mean that, but you must admit, Chief Inspector, we are under considerable strain." She hesitated. "I suppose that dreadful young man who rents the Workshop hasn't been taking her in? After all, she is still a young woman and pretty in a mad sort of way."

Miles looked furious. "And she is still my wife."

Emma glared at Vivian. "Cedric isn't a dreadful young man. He's my friend and—and not a bit like that."

"Dear me!" said Vivian, a spot of angry colour on each cheek. "We are touchy this morning."

"Think nothing of it," said Miles in a grim voice. "You ready, Emma?"

Before he could leave the room Finch remarked that he would like to take a look round the Lodge.

"Be my guest," said Miles, smirking and bowing extravagantly.

Vivian sighed. "You see what I mean? We *are* becoming peculiar."

"It's a difficult position," Finch conceded. "I'd be happier if we could lay our hands on that pistol.".

"You think it may be upstairs?" Vivian was pulling on a pair of pigskin gloves as she spoke. "I wish you luck."

The bedroom assigned to Harriet had been redecorated for her return home. For all its charm it had an unused, impersonal air. The bed had not been slept in. The dressing table was bare except for a silver-backed brush and comb. In the roomy wardrobe hung a few forlorn black robes.

"Unnatural, ain't they?" said Mrs. Partridge from the doorway. "Mr. Miles has ordered her two more, only in bright colours. One cherry red and the other shell pink, both colours she used to wear, so I'm told. He hopes that if they're hung up with the others, she may take to them. But I don't know, I'm sure."

"It must be an extraordinary household to work for," Finch commented, hopefully abandoning his search in favour of a gossip.

"You're right there. And it's changed a lot since Mrs. Miles came home."

"Changed? In what way?"

"I'm told that before that dreadful accident Mr. Miles used to be very lively and jolly. I've never known him like that but he could be depended upon for a smile and a few words of greeting. Now he seems to have turned in on himself, as you might say. Sometimes he'll sit glowering at nothing for half an hour on end. Fair gives me the creeps. Not that I altogether blame him, seeing how she avoids him. It seems as if she right down hates him—and I've never yet heard him speak a harsh word to her."

"About these articles Mrs. Miles has taken out of the house?"

"I know nothing about them. It's true Mr. Miles did ask me to try and find out what she'd done with them but when I asked her she just stared at me and answered not a word."

The search of Harriet's room did not take long. Nothing of any interest was found. Nor was Miles' room any more revealing. The two detectives went downstairs to the big sitting room. It was a man's room, comfortable and pleasantly untidy.

Finch threw a speculative glance at a large desk. He sat down in front of it and began a thorough examination of its contents.

There were receipts, bills, old invitations. Finch raised an eyebrow at the sum of Miles' gambling losses and spared a thought for the unwisdom of rich, doting fathers.

Finch found a pocket diary. Miles had kept it for nine months, recording his social engagements. He had been co-driver in a car rally. He had motored up to York for the horse racing. He had flown to Paris to dine with friends, to Cowes in a friend's yacht. Anything but work as an anodyne to grief.

On Sunday, September 29, there was a solitary sentence.

"Harriet came back."

After that the pages remained blank. Finch looked at the single entry with dismay.

Harriet came back.

He did not know why but those three words recorded in Miles' diary lingered in his mind disquietingly as the police car bore him and Sergeant Hollis to the big house.

A frightened-looking housemaid opened the front door.

"Nothing wrong with Mr. Grant, I hope?" Finch remarked.

The girl smiled uncertainly. "Chef says he's breaking up, but then he's ever so old."

Finch interviewed Miss Walters in the servants' hall. She was a thin, angular woman with a quiet voice and, Finch was glad to observe, a sensible intelligent face. She was still unnaturally pale.

"I'm sorry I couldn't see you last night," she said, "but I was upset." Miss Walters added grimly, "Made quite a spectacle of myself, I don't doubt."

"I'm not surprised that you were upset," Finch assured her. "Not many people would have done what you did."

"I went through with it because Mr. Theodore asked me to. And then Mrs. Buckler had always been so fastidious. It was shocking to see her like that. All wet and bedraggled and laying her out didn't seem so bad at the time. Not even when that police surgeon shouted at me. As if I would know the rules of *his* nasty occupation. No, it was later I got the horrors. It just came over me. And then this morning there's Mr. Theodore dead and Mrs. Miles gone no one knows where, the poor thing, never realising what she had done."

"Yes, it's a bad business. I suppose you saw Mrs. Buckler after that set-to she had with her daughter-in-law on the Friday? What was the first you heard of it?"

"It was when Mr. Geoffrey helped her up to her bedroom and rang for me."

"He *helped* her up?"

"When I got to her, Mrs. Buckler was lying on the bed, shivering and shaking, white as a ghost. I fancy it was the first time she'd ever been brought in contact with physical violence. I turned on the electric blanket and got her into bed with a couple of hot-water bottles for good measure, while Mr. Geoffrey went off to ring up Dr. Russel. She soon stopped trembling and lay, her head on a pile of pillows, her eyes fixed on the door,

watching for Mr. Theodore but he didn't come. I reckon
he was too angry with her."

"Mrs. Buckler was genuinely attached to her husband?"

Miss Walters smiled bleakly. "She liked having her
own way better, as she proved when the doctor came.
She caught at his hand and said, 'I haven't killed him,
have I?' And when Dr. Russel said it had been a near
thing and warned her that one more upset like that
would probably prove fatal, she said, 'How can it be
avoided while that dreadful young woman is at large?'
He answered her quite short and sharp. Mrs. Miles, he
said, presents no problems as long as she is not provoked. And with that Mrs. Buckler reared up in her
bed and cried out, 'So she is not to be provoked! And I,
am I not to be provoked?' Dr. Russel must have thought
he'd gone far enough, for between Mr. Buckler's ill-
health and Mrs. Buckler's fancies they must have been
among his most paying patients. He set to work to
soothe her down and before he left he gave her something to make her sleep."

"And next day?"

"She met with a general air of disapproval, which
wasn't very fair because Mrs. Buckler was genuinely
frightened of her daughter-in-law, and she got no sympathy." Miss Walters added caustically, "The only person who agreed with her in thinking Mrs. Miles was
dangerous was that nasty sly girl she planted on young
Mrs. Geoffrey."

"You mean Dora Short?"

"Yes. Originally Mrs. Buckler meant her for Mrs.
James, who was looking for a parlourmaid. When she
wouldn't take her, Mrs. Buckler passed her on to Mrs.
Geoffrey."

"But why find one at all?"

"Mrs. Buckler was someone who liked to know what
was going on. She didn't care for any of her husband's
family and never missed an opportunity to make
mischief—only she had to have the ammunition to do it
with."

"Had you been with her long?"

"Ever since she first arrived in this country. But if you're going to ask whether I liked her, then the answer is no. Foreign she was and foreign she remained. And she ought to have known how it would be being a third wife. I don't mean that Mr. Theodore neglected her, for he didn't. No, it was his fondness for. his family she couldn't stand."

"Had she any cause for complaint?"

"There's no denying Mr. Theodore indulged them in every way. They walked in and out of this house as if it were an hotel. They helped themselves to the wine out of the cellars. Or started Chef off cooking for some party Mrs. James might be giving. She was a great one for thinking up all sorts of things to annoy her mother-in-law."

"Such as having a list of the guests invited to last night's fireworks party?"

"Did Mrs. James have that? Well, that was the way it was. Remarkably aggravating, Mrs. James could be. Like encouraging Mrs. Miles to come into this house when she knew the mistress couldn't abide her near."

"Mrs. Miles' return hasn't been a success. I can see that. What I haven't been able to find out is what the late Mrs. Buckler was really like. A good hostess, a careful housekeeper, a devoted, if jealous, wife. None of that is very revealing. Even jealousy is common enough."

Miss Walters nodded. "I suppose I knew her better than most," she agreed. "She was one of those soft-spoken, very feminine-seeming women who are really as hard as steel—and she cried so freely that it was easy to underestimate her, particularly these last few months. She used to go to endless trouble to find out something bad about one of Mr. Theodore's two elder sons. Then she'd rush off and tell him. He'd be cross with her and maybe have a near heart attack. She'd cry and promise never to spy on them again, then she'd come up here and I'd brush her hair. She had lovely long dark hair and she found it soothing to have it brushed. After a little I'd see her face, reflected in the mirror, grow hard and scheming and I'd know she was at it again."

"You mentioned 'these last few months.' What had changed?"

"The mistress had changed her tactics. I think because she could see how bad these constant upsets were for Mr. Theodore's heart but the change worried Mr. James, I know. He never trusted her, although on the surface they seemed on quite good terms. He'd always been careful to be polite to her and so had Mr. Miles, but that didn't make any difference to Mrs. Buckler's feelings. She hated them both. I remember she once said to me, 'I can wait. In the end they'll come crawling to me. Crawling and grovelling on their knees.'"

Finch raised an eyebrow. "Strong words, weren't they?"

"I think it was because Mrs. Buckler had been used to having her own way. She couldn't believe that in time she wouldn't get what she wanted."

"I see. And what were her feelings towards Mr. Wheatley?"

"They got on very well together, which was lucky, seeing how much she had seen of him these last few months. Mr. Theodore's health being what it was, he'd send Mr. Philip to escort her to the theatre or to parties."

"Mr. Wheatley, I understand, was the son of Mr. Theodore's sister?"

"Widowed sister," Miss Walters corrected. "Mr. Theodore kept the pair of them. Paid for his schooling and then took him into the business. Mr. James and Mr. Miles never let him forget it. They'd leave Mr. Philip to do everything for Mr. Theodore. And it wouldn't surprise me if, when the will comes to be read, they don't come to regret it."

Finch nodded. "One last question. Did Mrs. Buckler seem any different before the party yesterday?"

"Oh, there was something going on. Or so she thought. She'd been in a state of suppressed excitement since the Monday evening. Then on the Tuesday morning she

could scarcely bring herself to stand still while I got her
ready to go out shopping. Not that I paid much attention. I'd seen her before when she thought she was
going to get the better—"

The woman's voice faltered. She looked at Finch, the
last remaining colour draining from her face. "Oh, my
God! You think that this time she really had found
something?"

When Finch had finished with Miss Walters he
suggested, to his sergeant's delight, that they should
have a look at Theodore Buckler's collection of carved
ivory.

"It would be in here, sir," said Hollis, opening a
door. "The big drawing room." Adding apologetically, "I
haven't seen it but I did ask Mr. Grant, who knows I am
interested in antiques, where the collection was kept."

The two men halted involuntarily, caught by the
beauty of the room, from the three eighteenth-century
chandeliers twinkling and shining as they hung from
the ceiling, to the soft colours of the enormous Aubusson
carpet on the floor.

Hollis gave a low whistle. "Sorry, sir—but that carpet! It must have cost a fortune."

"As, by the look of them, did most of the things in
this room." Finch was ambling slowly down it as he
spoke. He halted before one of the cabinets and looked
at his sergeant. "Well, Hollis? Here it is. Now, what do
you know?"

Hollis grinned. "Very little, sir." He was, with the
change in his fortunes, becoming a different man.

Finch had been staring in at the collection. "Is it my
imagination or does ivory vary in colour?"

"It varies with its place of origin. Ivory from what
used to be Ceylon, turns a pale pink. Thailand ivory
turns yellow, while that from West Africa becomes
whiter with time. The Egyptians actually dyed their
ivory different colours in baths of mineral salts."

"And what animals provide the ivory?"

"In the northern countries of Europe it was mostly

walrus tusks. Walruses and elephants provide the best ivory. Further south they get it from mammoths, walruses, elephants, hippopotamuses, and something called a narwhal." He added, "Objects were made in ivory twenty thousand years ago. At one time people believed that the stuff came from the horn of the unicorn."

Finch nodded. "Symbols of virginity."

"Yes, sir. It explains why so many religious objects made of ivory were consecrated to the Virgin. In medieval days ivory was thought to come from the mysterious land of the Queen of Sheba."

"That was a nice thought, too."

"Yes, sir. But it wasn't all romance." Hollis glanced uncertainly at Finch. Suppose he were talking too freely and all this wonderful collaboration were to cease? "I came across something that seemed right up our street," he ventured.

"Then let's hear it," said Finch.

"It seems, sir, that there were once three great families of elephants. I forget the Latin name of the one I mean, but it was also known as the woolly mammoth, because of its thick coat of coarse black hair. Every now and again one of these creatures is dug up in Siberia, so perfectly refrigerated that wolves, dogs and even men can eat the flesh with enjoyment. In 1937 at Wrangel Island off the coast of northeast Siberia, one was discovered in its entirety. And after all those thousands of years it actually still had an undigested meal in its stomach."

Finch was amused. "I see what you mean," he commented with a chuckle. "Wonder what Dr. Barnet would make of it if he were asked to give the time of death? Come to think about it, isn't there some mystery as to how these beasts perished?"

"Yes, sir. Some authorities suggest that they stepped into a bog and their own weight took them down. Of course not all at the same time. Others think that some sudden and unforeseen catastrophe overwhelmed them. No one really knows."

Finch had been looking at the collection of jewel cabinets, chessmen, drinking horns, mirror cases and religious objects. "And that," he said, pointing, "should be the 'Annunciation' the librarian told you about." He became aware that Grant had come into the room. "Good morning," he said. "I'm glad to see you. I was afraid that perhaps you were ill."

"No, sir—although I confess I did not get up as early as usual." Grant hesitated, then said, "Is there any news of poor Mrs. Miles? I did hope that when the police came and searched the house she would have been found hiding somewhere on the premises."

"There is no news. It begins to look as if she must have left the district."

"I can't think it likely, sir," Grant said. "At one time she was a great one for going about with Mr. Miles but since her breakdown this has been her world. She knows no other." He shook his head. "Dearie me, it's a sad business. The master would have been greatly upset—as we all are, particularly poor Mr. Miles." He walked towards the two detectives. "I think as I entered I heard you mention the 'Annunciation.' If I may say so, it is the one piece that is a fake."

Finch felt a thrill of pleasurable anticipation. "A fake?" he echoed—and managed to look surprised.

Grant smiled faintly. "We did have the original but a substitution took place during the time the house was let furnished."

"I didn't know the house had ever been let furnished."

"It was during Mr. Theodore's world cruise in search of renewed health. He knew that he would be away some time, so he decided that it would be better to let the house rather than have it stand empty. It also kept the staff occupied, which is always desirable. It was let, of course, only to very wealthy gentlemen and therein perhaps lay the danger. Very wealthy gentlemen, if I may say so, being unaccustomed to being thwarted."

"That sounds a very reasonable supposition. When was the theft discovered?"

"About two months after Mr. Theodore's return with the new mistress. A gentleman came here to luncheon who was a world authority on the art of the thirteenth and fourteenth centuries. It was he who discovered the substitution. Mr. Theodore was very angry. His first thought was to put the matter in the hands of the police, but on reflection he decided that it would not be worth the unpleasantness that must follow, not to mention the difficulty of bringing the theft home to anyone."

So that was the answer, Finch thought. That was why Consuelo had been so certain that eventually she would catch either James or Miles engaged in some malpractice. And that suggested further that, while she had probably been present when the theft of the "Annunciation" had been discovered, it was equally probable that as soon as her husband had known the truth of the matter, he had refused to discuss it further with her, or to disclose which of his sons had been responsible.

"Was the 'Annunication' stolen from the cabinet?" he asked.

"No, sir. We have a strong room. The 'Annunciation,' along with the cream of the master's collection was put in there."

"Who knows how to open it?"

"Only the members of the master's family and Mr. Judd, the family solicitor. It's that which makes it difficult to understand how the theft of the 'Annunciation' came about."

"Yes, indeed," Finch murmured. Evidently in Grant's mind there was a great difference between debts and common or garden theft. "Is there much kept in the strong room?"

"No, sir. When the master retired, everything in there was cleared out. Some went to the head office. Some to Mr. Judd." Grant looked about him sadly. "If I may be permitted to say so, I never cared for the carved ivory, I much preferred the paintings. There's a Greuze and four panels by Boucher—they were much admired at functions." His voice grew tremulous. "Great days," he muttered. "Gone, all gone. It is difficult to believe."

"'Sic transit gloria mundi,'" Finch murmured.

"Exactly, sir. Was there anything else I can tell you?"

"Yes, these tenants? I imagine that they were visitors to this country?"

"Yes, sir, all but one. He was a North Country gentleman connected with the electrical trade. Then there was a gentleman from Texas. Very persistent, he was. He made the master several offers for the property. The idea was, I believe, that the house should be dismantled, shipped to the States and reassembled. Then there was a French gentleman who made champagne and a Persian gentleman of somewhat curious habits, temporarily resident in this country."

"A number of short lets? Yes, I see. That would certainly have made the recovery of the original 'Annunciation' more difficult."

The old butler sighed. "It does seem wrong that anyone should be allowed to get away with such a barefaced theft."

With which sentiment Finch was in entire agreement.

Finch and Bodkin had lunch together. They discussed the case while they waited for the first course to arrive. Bodkin was surprised at the failure to find Harriet. Since she was a nutter he had expected her, if not exactly to give herself up, then at least to be easily captured.

"Since Harriet has a gun, she may have shot herself accidentally," he said, ruminating aloud. "If she doesn't turn up soon, we'll have to arrange for an all-out search. Police, volunteers, dogs—the lot."

Finch, who had favoured an all-out search for that morning, remarked that someone might be hiding her. Adding, "If one has the perfect scapegoat one would tend to hang on to her."

Bodkin frowned. "Who d'you think would do a thing like that?"

"The same person whom Mrs. Buckler expected to meet yesterday evening."

"I'll get a search warrant for Philip Wheatley's flat and Carter's flat and shop," said Bodkin. "We may find

her that way. The houses on the estate have all been
searched, except for the Workshop."

"I'll have a look round there."

"As far as I'm concerned, the morning has been a
complete loss." Bodkin looked round for the waiter. He
was hungry and growing impatient. "Take that ten
pounds Consuelo Buckler paid Dora Short, the daily at
the Small House. I sent Topham to interview her—and
it was just as well I did. Geoffrey Buckler had given her
a week's wages in lieu of notice and told her to clear
out."

"Good for him."

"But not so good for us if we'd had to find her. It
seems that Mrs. Buckler saw her at the servant registry
office and took a fancy to her. Never even asked for
references—which was as well, seeing that she hasn't
got any."

"And so was eminently suited for Mrs. Buckler's
purpose."

"Do we know Mrs. B.'s purpose?"

"I fancy she must have wanted a spy in James Buckler's household. Not for any particular purpose but on
general principles—but Vivian Buckler was too sharp
for her. She wouldn't take her. Hence Dora's appearance at the Small House."

"Dora's story is that, on her way to work yesterday
morning, she was surprised to see James Buckler walking along in front of her. The time was then 7:50 A.M.
He went in by the small gate of The Elms and up
through the woods, with the girl following at a discreet
distance. When they reached the far side of the ridge
he began to measure up the land, writing down the
result of his calculations in a small notebook. Dora only
waited long enough to satisfy herself that he was not
expecting to be joined by anyone, then she went back
to her work at the Small House and phoned Mrs. B.,
who was delighted with Dora's news and later that
morning took her round the sum of ten pounds. She
was, Dora said, terrified in case she met Harriet."

Here the waiter brought two helpings of steak-and-kidney pudding, vegetables and two tankards of draught beer. Bodkin was silent for a time while he took the fine edge off his appetite.

"I saw James Buckler myself," the Superintendent said at last. "He was at The Grange. Philip Wheatley was there and they were expecting Miles. James admitted the truth of Dora's story. Said it had been obvious that his father could not last much longer and that the sooner some houses went up, the better for all. He said he planned to build smallish houses for the not-so-well-to-do. Made himself sound quite a philanthropist. He agreed that his stepmother had taxed him with going against his father's wishes. He declared that *he* was the one to come off best and that he'd given her a piece of his mind as a mischief-making bitch—which doesn't exactly tally with young Mrs. Geoffrey's tale." Bodkin shook a disapproving head. "A hard man, Mr. James."

"And we don't know that that was all Mrs. Buckler had against him," Finch pointed out. As Bodkin seemed not to be going to say anything further, he continued. "Some things are beginning to hang together. For instance, when Theodore Buckler went abroad in search of renewed health, as Grant so felicitously put it, he was the possessor of a valuable fourteenth-century carved-ivory 'Annunciation.' When he came back he found himself with only a fake. At the time, it put him out considerably."

Bodkin stopped eating. A slow grin spread over his ample face and narrowed his eyes. "So that was what I was supposed to have looked into. I've often wondered."

"Yes, although who was responsible for the substitution, I don't know. It was a crime anyone might have committed, provided they knew how to open the strong-room door. What isn't in doubt is that such a substitution took place. Imagine the position." Finch's gaze, like his voice, was mild and considering. "Theodore Buckler and his ever-open purse were on the other side of the world. Also he was at that time very much occupied with a fascinating widow and therefore not inclined to be interested in the welfare of his family. So one of them took the genuine 'Annunciation' to Justin Besson and had it copied—and to the sculptor there would have seemed nothing illegal in that. People do have their treasures copied. To foil thieves. To make a presentation. Or, as in this case, so that the original could be sold without causing speculation and comment. Besson could not have known."

"The French police said he was an honest man."

"But who bought the original? Personally I favour the Persian gentleman of curious habits and only temporarily resident in this country. I feel this last point must have weighed heavily with whoever it was who suddenly found himself short of money."

"That wouldn't have been James Buckler. He wasn't short of cash. He was fairly splashing it about on that fine new house—" The Superintendent's voice trailed away. When he spoke again it was to remark shortly that obviously no one could be counted out.

"As to what happened to Besson that Easter Monday, the fact that he hasn't been seen since tends to illumine the subject with a somewhat sinister light."

"But why kill him? Theodore Buckler knew all about the trick someone had played him," Bodkin pointed out.

"And yet someone did batter Justin Besson to death."

Bodkin was driven to protest. "Come, come! Without seeing the body, you can't know how he died."

"The blood," said Finch simply. He added, in his small voice, "Consider a moment. There are two maid-servants living in. As was customary they had been given the day off to go to the fair. But they would be back at—ten o'clock? Eleven? Plenty of time then to conceal the crime if the victim was just lying there neat and tidy. But if he wasn't? If there was blood about? A wrecked room, perhaps? Then the only solution was a fire. A great big beautiful destructive fire."

"And in Miles' house."

"Which doesn't seem as significant as it might have done. The Bucklers are a close-knit family. With them it's one for all and all for one." Finch added reflectively after a pause, "If I remember rightly we weren't told what brought Besson to this country?"

"I'll get in touch with Interpol and put the question to them. It may tell us something, cold though the trail is. It won't tell us why Mrs. B. was killed. D'you think *she* could have found out that Besson had been murdered—if he had?"

"A secret like that must have been dynamite. Particularly with a woman about of Consuelo Buckler's character. As to what put her on to it, could it have been the *In Memoriam* in the *Gazette*?"

"Can't see our Mrs. B. even knowing that the *Gazette* existed."

"There is that," Finch agreed, frowning thoughtfully. "The *Gazette* comes out on a Thursday and Miss Walters did say that her mistress' excitement dated from the Monday evening. On the Tuesday morning she was all impatience to go out—and it'll be useless to ask her chauffeur where she went. It won't be that easy. To my mind Consuelo was a born intriguante. Nor are her actions all of a piece. When Dora saw her she was terrified at the very thought of meeting her daughter-in-law Harriet. Yet that same evening she gave her guests the slip and went quite happily to the lonely far end of the lake."

"A stupid woman."

"But dangerous to someone."

The two men fell silent as the waiter brought each man a large helping of jam roly-poly. Finch eyeing it pensively, decided that a walk to the Workshop was the least he could do for his digestion.

"D'you think that whoever searched Mrs. B.'s bedroom found what he was looking for?"

"I know *we* didn't. Perhaps Consuelo took it with her on that clandestine outing—in which case Harriet may have it."

Bodkin looked up. "I don't like that. Harriet with a pistol is bad enough. Harriet with a pistol and the evidence of a murder in her possession—" He did not finish the sentence but shook his head disconsolately.

"With the Lodge open at all hours and one of the library windows at Westlea Park open last night, we can't be certain who was about. But there is something that does concern Harriet." Finch recounted how he had found Miles Buckler's diary with its final ambiguous entry.

The Superintendent refused to take this seriously. "Know what I think?"

"No, what?"

"That Harriet *has* come back." And Bodkin gave one of his loud guffaws.

Finch looked pensive. "Then perhaps you can tell me how Harriet, suffering from amnesia, comes to remember her hatred and fear of her husband?"

Bodkin answered Finch's question with another. "Ever thought how you'd feel if you were Harriet and found yourself sharing a house with a man you can't remember ever having seen before?"

In the afternoon Finch and Hollis were driven once more to Westlea Park. They left the car on the gravel sweep and walked towards the Small House. Before they reached it, Emma had come out wearing a black frock and coat and with a black chiffon scarf over her bright head. Neither man had seen her in a skirt before. They noted with approval that she had very nice legs, long and slim.

She saw them and waited.

"If you're going to the Workshop we'll walk with you." Finch added, "How did this morning's search go?"

"With Miles?" Emma frowned a little. "I do believe Vivian is right. We are becoming peculiar. Miles and I made quite a sensation when we arrived at the big pond—the police had already dragged the small one. Miles swore horribly when they brought up first an old bicycle and then part of a brass bedstead. But he wouldn't give up. We went all through the woods calling Harriet's name." Her voice shook a little. "We called and called but she never answered."

Finch looked at her curiously. "You do think she's
dead, don't you?"

"I can't see what else can have happened to her. I
mean, it's practically impossible to imagine Harriet
booking a room in an hotel. Or taking a train journey to
get away and hide." Emma sighed. She said in a low
voice, "I think in a way Harriet was always hiding.
Even walking into a lake would be a form of hiding,
wouldn't it?"

"Can she swim?"

Emma shook her head. "She'd just step into a hole
and drown."

They walked on in silence for a time. "I suppose the
loss of one's child is about the most traumatic experience a woman can undergo," Finch remarked.

"Poor Harriet just cried and cried. In fact she was so
distraught that no one but the staff were allowed near
her for nearly a whole week."

Finch looked at her in surprise. "But I understood
that Mrs. Miles went out of her mind when told that
her son was dead?"

"Oh, no! That came sometime later. Geoffrey, who
had flown home for Bunny's funeral, had been back in
France for several days when he had a letter from Dad
telling him that Harriet had had a complete breakdown
and had been put in a mental home."

In response to Finch's questioning, Emma worked
out the chronological record of Harriet's stay in the
Ilverstoke District Hospital.

"Let's see if I've got it right. The accident occurred
on Sunday, March 26?" he said.

"And poor Bunny's funeral was four days later. Then
Dad took Consuelo to the South of France, meaning to
stay for a couple of weeks, but they came home as soon
as they heard that The Elms had been burnt down.
That was on the Easter Monday—the fire I mean."

"That was April 3," said Finch, consulting a small
diary.

Emma sighed. "You do have to be accurate, don't
you?"

"Positively pedantic," Finch agreed. "Tell me, how did Philip get on with James and Miles?"

"Geoffrey says they've always made use of him. James calls it 'earning his keep.' Philip doesn't have to do it but I expect it's become a sort of habit." Emma went on, "Of course I'd only just met Geoffrey when Harriet went into a mental home but we've often discussed it since. We even brought up the subject with Dad but he didn't really know. He said that he supposed her grief was cumulative." Emma added gloomily, "I hope the same thing doesn't happen to me." She sighed deeply. "I can't help wishing that Harriet had shot Consuelo a day earlier. Then she wouldn't have sent us a hot plate. I wouldn't have asked for a divorce. Cedric wouldn't have taken me to the Green Man and perhaps Dad wouldn't be dead either."

Emma remembered that they should have been celebrating her father-in-law's birthday. Two large tears ran down her cheeks. She wiped them away, then blew her nose in a manly looking white handkerchief bordered in black.

"I don't think I care much for Cedric," said Finch meditatively.

"I like him," Emma answered, in a voice muffled by the handkerchief, "but sometimes I think he makes a bad situation worse just out of mischief."

Finch looked at her. "Things are no better with you?"

Emma shook her head. "You remember my telling you about that horrid little spare bedroom? Well, I'm still in it."

Finch nodded. For a man deeply in love, Geoffrey seemed oddly determined to get his wife to leave him.

They paced silently along for a while, Hollis a little behind them.

"Tell me," said Finch suddenly, "what made the late Mrs. Buckler interfere in your affairs?"

"She didn't call it interfering. She alluded to little deeds of kindness along life's way."

"Revolting," said Finch firmly.

"Of course I can see now that I ought to have made a

stand right at the beginning. I should have told her to get stuffed."

"Yes," said Finch solemnly. "You missed out there."

Emma gave a somewhat shaky chuckle. "D'you know the first thing Consuelo gave us? A solid-silver twister to use on toothpaste tubes. Geoffrey thought it was a joke but I had a feeling then that it was the beginning of trouble."

"Don't tell me you have the feminine habit of squeezing the tube in the middle?"

"Worse than that. I can never remember not to do it to Geoffrey's tube. I suppose because it always looks fatter than mine."

They had come now within sight of the Workshop. Emma felt in her pocket and produced a large old-fashioned key. She unlocked the door and stepped inside. With the ease of experience she parted the hangings to disclose a cupboard.

She hung her coat and scarf in it and put on an overall. "All the things here are for sale," she remarked, waving a hand vaguely around.

"What would you recommend? An owl with a clock in the centre of its stomach? Or a man's bald head on which I could grow grass?"

"The best thing to grow is cress. Then you can cut it for sandwiches," Emma advised. "And if you think these things pretty horrible, wait until you see the Frenchman." Adding shrewdly, "I suppose that *is* what you've come for?"

Finch nodded. "By all means, let us see the nasty Frog," he murmured, "although I can't believe that he can be worse than the things out here."

"To me he's much worse because he seems to have some curious life of his own. Sometimes I think that Monsieur Besson must be dead and that it's a case of demonic possession. When I'm here alone I put a cloth over his head so that he can't watch me." As she spoke Emma opened the door into the centre room. "There he is."

Finch looked at the figure with interest, hearing

Hollis, who was just behind him, catch his breath, half in recognition, half in excitement.

It stood against the wall yet seemed to dominate the room, the figure of a tall, thin, elderly man with a face furrowed in all directions. A grim, fanatical face, the thin lips sneering above a tuft of beard. The dark, almost uncannily living eyes, seeming to Finch to follow his movements with a sly, malign watchfulness.

"Real hair and expensive glass eyes?" Finch commented. "That hardly seems playing the game."

"The experts use what pleases them best. For instance Cedric likes white paper for his heads." Emma added with a touch of professional pride that amused Finch, "One roll of white toilet paper makes two pounds of pulp."

Finch turned to study the poster hanging on the wall beside the figure. It was some two feet square, on paper that simulated the yellowing of age. There was a photograph of the missing man. Under it was printed in large decorative type:

£100 Reward
The above sum will be paid to anyone whose information will lead to the discovery of the whereabouts, dead or alive, of Justin Besson who, when he disappeared, was 70 years of age. He was last seen at Victoria Railway Station at 10:45 A.M. on Monday, April 3, 1973.

Finch looked at his sergeant. "Seen this photograph before?"

"Yes, sir," Hollis was emphatic. "This has been made to look antique but it's the same photograph we had at the station."

Finch nodded, turned and looked once more at the Frenchman. "A remarkable likeness," he told Emma, adding, "Odd how the story has kept alive."

"It was going strong when I came to England five months ago," Emma answered.

"The poster has quite a Victorian appearance," Finch murmured politely. "True to the age of papier-mâché, I imagine."

Emma shook her head. "Papier-mâché is centuries old. Why, Chinese warriors of the Middle Ages used to wear helmets of the stuff, made on very much the same principle as today."

On a long trestle table in the centre of the room was the wire frame Cedric had made.

"That's going to be the basis of the second Frenchman. I'm going to do it, all but the head," said Emma, not without pride.

"You have more figures, no doubt?"

"Yes, they're through there." Emma nodded in the direction of another door. "The rest of the stock is in the attic. Do look around if you want to."

Finch took her at her word. He opened the door and found the room beyond dark and shadowy. He switched on the light and at once it sprang into view.

Here there had been no attempt at decoration. The walls were dingy, while decaying fragments of a once-expensive paper hung on them here and there. Faded curtains covered the only window. At the far end of the narrow room was an outer door. A dozen or so tall figures lined one wall, all, Finch thought, grinning most damnably.

"What d'you think of this little lot?" he asked Hollis in a low voice.

"I can't see why you should want one of these at a party."

"Possibly you could if you were young. A party presided over by Bacchus, Pan, Venus—" Finch noticed, as he spoke, that as well as bars to the window, the back door was locked, bolted, and further reinforced by a steel bar.

They went back to the other room, Hollis switching off the light behind them.

"An unholy brood," Finch remarked.

"It's only the young who hire them. They think it

sophisticated," said Emma, with a tolerant air. "It can't do them any harm."

"D'you mind if my sergeant looks upstairs?"

"Of course not. I only wish he would find Harriet there."

"I don't expect her to be here now," Finch murmured. "I just wondered if there were any signs that she *had* been here."

Chapter Six

A small green van came bucketing up the rough track towards the Workshop. A minute later Cedric Carter entered the room. His eyes were very bright, his glance both inquisitive and shrewd.

"Good afternoon, Chief Inspector. Afternoon, Sergeant. I hope your wife is well?"

Finch glancing at Hollis saw him stiffen.

"I didn't know that you knew my wife."

"The fair Marion? Yes, I knew her. Not that I was ever a suitor for her hand. In those days, not so long ago after all, I couldn't have supported a wife. Still, give her my regards. Tell her—" Cedric caught Hollis' hostile gaze and added airily, "No, tell her nothing." He turned to Emma with an air, assumed Finch felt sure, of one anxious to cover up feelings of confusion and embarrassment. "Emma, sweet child, hasn't anyone told you that we don't wear black in this country?"

Emma gave him a severe look. "In France we wear it to show that we are mourning. I am mourning for Dad."

Cedric smiled at her. "I'm not complaining, chick. I

always did think black stockings were sexy. And yours look sexier than most." He turned back to Finch. "What can I do for you? Although I must tell you that the police have already been here. A futile exercise I'm afraid. What with locks and bars, wayward Harriet hadn't a chance of hiding in here."

"Locks and bars? You have a problem with vandals?"

"That's right. The place isn't so near the road, but in the summer you get teen-agers trespassing all over this side of the ridge, and my papier-mâché figures are irreplaceable. Still, it was the previous owner of Westlea Park who was responsible for the bolts and bars. I only keep them in repair."

"Has Harriet Buckler ever been in here?"

"Never."

"But I suppose you have seen her sometimes in the woods?"

"I've seen her once or twice but not for long. She is as shy of strangers as a wild doe. In fact, now I come to think about it, she behaves just like one. If I go near her she backs away, her eyes fixed on me, then suddenly she'll turn and make off."

"Did you see her at any time yesterday?"

Cedric shook his head. "I wish I had, poor creature."

Finch glanced at the figure of the Frenchman and had a queer impression that its gaze had only that moment been removed. He indicated the poster. "How did you come by that photograph of Justin Besson?"

"Photograph?" Cedric shook his head. "And yet I must admit that I did inadvertently see a photograph of the man one day when I had reason to call at the police station. It depicted such a strange wolfish face that it stuck in my mind. I came back and made a papier-mâché copy, which turned out so well that I photographed the result and used it for the poster. That too came out rather well, wouldn't you agree?"

"Except for a slight discrepancy," Finch answered dryly. "On the poster, as in reality, Besson had a small scar near the hairline over his left temple. It is absent on the papier-mâché head. So I ask you again, how did you come by that photograph?"

Cedric Carter continued to smile, although Finch could see that he was annoyed at being caught out.

"Come, come, Chief Inspector! You wouldn't expect me to betray my sources." His smile vanished, to be replaced by a look of genuine anxiety. "Here, you're not trying to find Justin Besson, as well as Harriet?"

"Why not?"

"Because if you do, a very profitable part of my income will dry up."

"I shall live for the day," said Finch pleasantly.

Cedric Carter watched through the window as the two detectives walked away up the ridge. "I do believe the fellow means it," he muttered angrily.

Emma emerged from a large cupboard, clasping a pile of old newspapers to her chest. "Means what?"

"Means to find the Frenchman."

"But you've always said that he never came here," said Emma, dumping the newspapers on the centre table.

"That was business." Cedric caught her outraged eye. He added hurriedly, "I would have told you. It was often on the tip of my tongue, only it seemed wiser to keep it to myself. You have such a yearning to do the right thing. I know you'll grow out of it but just at present you'd have been certain to tell your husband and in no time the police would have been poking about."

"Well, you've got them now," Emma declared with considerable satisfaction.

"Too true." Cedric turned away from the window. He perched on one of the high stools which stood about. "The whole thing sprang from a chance remark of mine," he explained airily. "I was just starting this lark. Experimenting, beginning to realise that what caught on with the kids was the macabre, the way-out thing. Then one evening I went to my local, the Bunch of Grapes, and there was this chap I knew, Detective Sergeant Topham, sitting alone and looking as sour as vinegar. Now I'm not one for glooming, but for some reason I took my drink over to his table. I asked what was needling him and he told me it was Sergeant Hollis. That Interpol were inquiring after a missing Frenchman and that Hollis claimed to have seen him on the Easter Monday in Grove Drive. I said, 'In that crowd? Don't make me laugh,' at which Topham put down his tankard and sat staring straight in front of him as if he'd seen a vision. 'That's it,' he said. 'Ridicule! If we could think of some way of making his claim seem ludicrous, we could kill it stone dead!'"

Emma looked at Cedric ironically. It might have happened like that. On the other hand it might not. "Only you didn't kill it stone dead, did you? You kept it alive so that you could make money out of it."

Cedric sighed. "I knew you wouldn't understand."

"Too right, I wouldn't. And what has this Topham against Sergeant Hollis?"

"He and Hollis joined the police force at about the same time. They were both smart but Topham got the idea that Hollis was preferred to him. Actually I could have told him that he was a lot *too* smart and too fond of bending the truth to suit himself."

"And did you really know Mrs. Hollis?"

"I knew her before he did."

"I suppose what you mean is that you were taking her about when Sergeant Hollis came along and cut you out."

Cedric looked sulky. "I didn't know that she was looking for a husband. If I had I wouldn't have bothered with her."

Emma nodded. That was like Cedric. The whole thing was like Cedric. His self-esteem had been hurt by Hollis and he had gone to fantastic lengths to punish him for it.

"But if the Frenchman were found, wouldn't the demand for his effigy be even greater?"

Cedric shook his head moodily. "People only like to imagine gruesome things. Not for them to actually take place."

"What do you think really happened to the Frenchman?"

Cedric shrugged. "What would you think had happened to a man who was seen and recognised eighteen months ago in broad daylight on a busy road—and then was neither seen nor heard of again?"

Emma was conscious of a sudden inward shiver. It was as if a cold wind had blown in from somewhere. She had been cutting a newspaper into long three-inch strips. Now she threw down her scissors. "At least Harriet wasn't responsible for that. She was still in hospital. Oh, I do wish we had never begun this conversation," she cried unhappily.

Cedric nodded gloomily. "Remembering Pandora's box, Bluebeard's last wife, and other inquisitive chicks even nearer home, it does seem to have been a bit of a mistake."

He stood up and reached for his coat. He glanced at the bold white face of the cheap clock on the mantelpiece. "It's a quarter to four now. I'll be back by five or just after. If you wait and give me a hand getting the stock into the attic, I'll see you home."

Emma agreed. She followed him to the door and watched him climb into his van. She waved, then turned back into the house. She went into the centre room where the Frenchman's strangely glinting eyes seemed to be watching for her return.

She walked over and stood in front of him. She had thought that, seeing him with the eyes of pity, he might appear different but he did not. Baleful he had always appeared and baleful he remained.

Sighing, Emma went back to her work. She took up one of the newspaper strips. She folded over one side halfway to the centre. She brushed it with paste and folded over the other side. She now had a strip three layers thick and almost an inch wide. She took up the wire frame Cedric had fashioned, and wound a strip about one arm like a bandage. She repeated the process again and again until she had built up a firm and well-shaped arm.

The work occupied her hands. It did nothing to control her thoughts. She turned over in her mind the few meagre facts told her by Cedric.

She wondered how Besson had died—for no one could disappear for so long and not be dead, she reflected, at least not in England. Perhaps he had been knocked down and, in falling, had struck his head on something solid and so killed himself. His assailant, she told herself, must then have panicked and hidden the body.

Emma stopped working. Her thoughts were beginning to frighten her. Buried, she decided after a moment. That would have been the only possibility. She did not, as Finch had done, think of the burnt-out Elms. Instead she seemed to see a mound, long and narrow, in some lonely part of the woods where the sun never penetrated.

She recalled, shuddering, that Geoffrey had told her that Dad had seemed to have something on his mind. Geoffrey had attributed it to the fancies of a very sick man. But suppose he had known or suspected the truth about the Frenchman's disappearance?

Someone knocked on the outer door.

Emma looked up, alarmed. Who could it be? Harriet, if she knocked at all, would not have done so with such assurance. Miles or James would just have walked in.

"Come in," she called. "The door isn't locked." She heard quick light footsteps cross the floor of the outer room. The door opened and Philip stood there, smiling and smoothing back his wind-blown hair. He looked out of place, she thought, very sleek and citified in a dark suit and an expensive short raincoat.

She stared at him in astonishment. "Philip! What are you doing here?"

"I was walking past, when I thought of you."

"But you never do walk through the woods."

"I can't think why. When I haven't the car it's quite the quickest way home."

"Once out of the woods Waterloo House is almost

opposite," Emma agreed, trying to pin down the change she sensed in him.

"I've been at The Grange since half past nine, listening to the family arguing. At half past three I couldn't stand it any more. I just walked out," said Philip surprisingly.

"James usually gets his own way in the end. What was the argument about?"

"The question was whether to have a private or a public funeral for Uncle Theodore. James pointed out that in the former the mourners would be swamped by sight-seers and ghouls. While with the latter, with friends, representatives of the borough council, of companies and charities in which Uncle had been interested, the very number and status of the mourners would serve to keep the rabble at a distance. Geoffrey, who had wanted a family funeral, saw the truth of what James had said, but Miles—well, you know him. Obstinate as a mule. He just kept saying 'No' over and over until I was afraid I'd kick him. So—I came away."

Emma had been listening with a fascinated attention. She could quite imagine Philip wanting to kick Miles— he must often have wanted to do so—but to actually *say* it! Mentally she shook a wondering head.

Philip took up one of the crumpled tubes. "What on earth are these?"

"They are—or were before I spoilt them—the basis for a hand. You run a thick wire into each tube, put an elastic band round one end, and thrust that end into the empty arm socket."

"Well, it's a way of passing the time."

"Don't be so patronising." Emma reflected that she had heard Cedric say that he hated Theodore's three sons for what they had and James and Miles for what they were, arrogant, purse-proud bastards. Philip, for the first time, sounded a little like the last two.

He was, she saw, staring around. There was about him an air of high expectancy. His gaze fell on the figure of the Frenchman. Emma heard him catch his breath. "Besson!" he said—and it was almost a whisper.

"Why did you say his name like that?"

Philip turned to look at her. "Like what?"

"As if you knew him."

Philip laughed easily. "Is that what I sounded like? I can assure you I never knew him. It was just that your friend Carter has made him something of a celebrity." He moved towards the door. "Well, I must be going. Uncle Theodore's death is going to make a lot of work for me."

Emma followed him. "Is Geoffrey still at The Grange?"

"He was when I left. You know Geoffrey. A tower of strength in time of trouble. And Miles *is* trouble."

Emma stood at the front door. A tower of strength to everyone but me, she thought desolately. She became aware that already the early dusk was falling. Philip had gone from sight. There was nothing now but the chill November wind blowing past. Shivering a little, she turned back into the building.

In the shadowy room the Frenchman's face had taken shape against the darkening wall behind him. Indeed it stood out—almost as if he had altered his position, moved forward a few paces, furtively, silently, while she had been seeing Philip off.

Obeying a sudden impulse, she picked up the figure. She carried it into the end room. There was a space between Pan and Apollo. She stood it there.

The fading light seemed to make the shabby red curtains glow. It flickered in the Frenchman's eyes. A wandering draught from the ill-fitting window moved the curtains and stirred his hair. Meeting his bleak derisive stare, Emma had a momentary fear that he was about to speak.

That would be true horror, she thought. Something quite ordinary, man-made and inanimate, suddenly executing a purely human movement. A slow word. A step on the floor. Worst of all to look up and find him at one's elbow.

She went back into the central room and switched on

all the lights. She began to make a second hand. Outside, the storm seemed to be getting progressively more violent. The wind buffeted the walls and screamed across the roof.

It was nearly six when the small van returned. Cedric came in carrying a cardboard box in each hand. He looked strained and angry.

"What has been happening?" Emma asked. "Did you have a breakdown?"

Cedric gave her a goaded look. "You may well ask. The police searched my flat, the shop and the workroom— by order of your friend the Chief Inspector. The kids were furious."

"But could the police do that?"

"They had search warrants."

Emma looked at him in dismay. "How beastly," she said slowly.

"The Chief Inspector seemed to think that Harriet might be there. Sergeant Topham, who was in charge of the operation, told me that everyone else except that fellow, Hollis, is certain that she is dead. He says it's the inescapable conclusion, and I'm inclined to agree with him."

"It does seem the most likely explanation," said Emma sadly. "Otherwise, why has no one seen her?" She followed Cedric out to the van. "Philip was here this afternoon. Wasn't it queer? He spoke Besson's name as if he had known him."

Cedric's brow darkened. He put down the boxes he had been carrying. "Let's get this straight, Emma. You must try not to give Besson another thought. And don't mention him to anyone. *Not anyone*. You might easily talk to the wrong person. James, for instance."

Emma was perplexed. "But James hasn't shown any interest in the Frenchman."

"No, but his lackey has. You've just told me so."

Emma, taking a couple more boxes from the van, reflected that "lackey" was just what Philip had seemed not to be. She said aloud, "I did think of that. I mean I did think that someone in the family might have killed

Monsieur Besson. Only," her voice pleaded, "I thought it might have been accidental."

"Accidental, my foot!" Cedric brought in some more boxes. "That's the lot." He went into the other room. He came back carrying Emma's outdoor clothes. He buttoned her into her coat and tied the scarf over her head. "We'll leave the boxes where they are. The van likewise. Now I'm going to walk you home. When you get there, stay there. You can't help anyone. You may easily make things worse. And just bear this in mind. Where two people have been murdered, there really is no reason not to add a third."

Emma looked at him in horror. "Two people? But what connection could there be between Consuelo's death and that of Monsieur Besson?"

"I don't know—and that's how I like it." Cedric looked at her searchingly. "You're looking a bit peaky. Would you rather come into West Ilverstoke and have dinner there? No one would know you. We could live it up a bit."

Emma shook her head. "I keep hoping that Geoffrey will have missed me. I'd rather go home."

Cedric nodded. He tucked her arm through his. "Perhaps that would be best. The kids were so angry with the fuzz that they may make a bit of bother. You wouldn't like that."

Emma knew Cedric's creed. An eye for an eye. She did not approve but she felt too depressed to argue with him.

They set out, Cedric hurrying her along. He had not the assurance of which she had been so comfortably aware when walking with the Chief Inspector. He was tense, fearful. No longer even very friendly. Emma's spirits sank still further.

The wild crashing of branches overhead, the uncertain light, the few last leaves whirling past, gave an air of unreality to the scene. It was like a Wagnerian opera, loud, grandiose and awesome.

"Cedric, I know you don't like Philip," she said at last, shouting, her mouth close to his ear, "but you'd have liked him still less this afternoon. For the first time he reminded me of James. He told me he nearly kicked Miles. And he actually walked out of The Grange without permission."

To her surprise, Cedric paused, swinging round to face her. Peering at him, she saw that he looked delighted. "So Uncle Theodore has done the right thing by him," he shouted gleefully. "If it's shares in the company, there'll be a power struggle worth seeing."

Emma's own spirits rose in sudden contrast to the miseries of the day. "It will be a battle of Titans," she cried.

"Which James will win."

"If not James, then Vivian."

"You're right. Never underestimate a nose like Vivian's."

They walked on, hands clasped, laughing wildly, staggering against the wind.

They were within sight of the Small House when Emma spoke. "Cedric, you don't think that Philip—?"

Cedric's face stiffened. "I don't think anything. Neither do you."

When Emma went into the house there was a light on in Geoffrey's room. The door was open and he was sitting at his desk.

"Did Cedric bring you back?" he asked, looking across to where she stood uncertainly in the doorway. "That was good of him."

Emma's heart sank at his tone of cool indifference. "Wasn't it horrid? The police searched his shop and the flat, thinking that Harriet might be there."

"And she wasn't? Too bad." Geoffrey added dismissively, "I've left you a meal in the dining room. Only cold, I'm afraid—but then I didn't know when you would be back."

"Aren't you having it with me?"

"I'm not hungry—and I have some work to do." He was feeding a sheet of paper into the typewriter. Then, "I've been with James and that's put me off food for now. Poor chap! He's upset. He got Judd to tell him the contents of Dad's will. It seems he made a new one two months after getting home. Judd said that he knew that Consuelo wouldn't want to stay in England if anything happened to him, so he left Westlea Park to James—but only for his life. After that it's to go, suitably endowed, to the National Trust."

"Oh dear! James should never—"

"Have tried to build those houses up on the ridge? I agree."

"Do you mind very much?"

"If it weren't for James, I'd think it a good idea."

"I think it a good idea." Emma reflected despairingly how stilted they both sounded. As if they were strangers making conversation. "Philip called at the Workshop. He seemed very cheerful."

"He had reason to be. Dad left him a large block of shares in the company," said Geoffrey shortly. He began to type. As Emma was leaving the room, he raised his voice a little to halt her. "I think that as soon as practicable you'd better go back to France. You still have the cottage at Collioure. Or you could go somewhere else. Suit yourself."

Emma made no reply. Her eyes filled with tears. How had she come to laugh with Cedric? That she had done so seemed incredible now. She wandered almost blindly into the dining room. She had no appetite. The charming familiarity of the green and white colour scheme surrounded her with a terrible sense of doom.

She pushed back her chair and went upstairs to the hated small spare bedroom. She did not turn on the light but went to the window. She stood there looking mournfully out to where the treetops lashed themselves distractedly to and fro.

She thought of Dad. She knew that he had looked on himself only as a custodian of Westlea Park.

She thought of Harriet. Was Topham right? Was she dead? Had she thrown herself into the lake?

She did not think of Geoffrey. That way lay despair.

The moon came and went, obscured by racing clouds. A policeman passed below her. She saw his expression, alert, purposeful, as he glanced in at a lighted downstairs window. He went on towards the big house and was soon out of sight.

Emma frowned, pressing her face closer to the glass. She had an oblique view in the distance of the woods surrounding The Elms. There something—or someone— was moving. Moving out from the trees. Crossing an open space so that, for a moment she had a clear view.

Harriet! It was Harriet. Not in her cloak but in one of the long dark robes she wore habitually. She glided across the grass quickly and with something of a furtive air, to disappear in the dark opening of the path leading past the ruined Elms.

For some moments after she had gone from sight Emma stood where she was, staring and bemused. It was not possible, she thought. And what seemed not possible was that Harriet appeared just as usual, neither hunted nor drooping with fatigue. And certainly she was not dead.

Emma's heart warmed to her sister-in-law. So miraculously preserved and so innocently wandering in what had become a threatening world.

Emma switched on the centre light in the bedroom. She snatched a dark anorak from the cupboard and ran down the stairs. She took some time to find Geoffrey's powerful car torch, one he had bought to take with him when motoring in lonely countries abroad. It shone with a broad beam of clear light. It also, if needed, shone red. Emma let herself out of the house and hurried down the path and up the pasture land on the further side. Harriet had had a good start, but now that Emma knew that she was alive she was determined to find her.

The night seemed enormous about her. Everything in sight was in motion, branches, bushes, briars, grass. Emma's clothes blew out, then moulded themselves to her figure. Long strands of hair escaped from the pins and straggled across her face.

She came to the path and pushed her way through the hole in the hedge. Once in the overgrown garden she stood still, turning her light this way and that, hearing, with faint uneasiness, the creak and scrape of the ancient elms above her.

She walked on, more slowly now, reflecting that it would be of little use to call Harriet by name, since the noise of the storm would drown her voice. She halted, thinking that someone had called out. "It was only the wind," she said aloud, and laughed a little to reassure herself.

Not completely confident, she turned off the light. What its beam did most successfully, she thought, was to make her position obvious to—whoever had called out. That is, if anyone had called.

After a little the darkness appeared to thin. She could make out the two walls black as night. A bit of star-hung sky showed through the now-leafless trees.

Suddenly the blood was chilled in her veins. Close by her, almost at her feet it seemed, had come a groan, a low sighing groan of one as much in sorrow as in pain.

Emma switched on the light. Its broad beam lay across the crumbling path and crept up the once-pale walls. She flashed it around. There was no one to be seen.

The groan came again, louder, and, Emma thought, very disturbing to hear. She walked round the broken wall, her shadow running before her across the ruined floor. She nearly trod on someone lying on the other side.

It was Miles. As she dropped on her knees beside him she met with a shock. She thought she saw the pale glint of eyeballs where she had expected the lids to be closed. She bent lower and saw that she had been mistaken. His eyes *were* closed. She saw too that he had three long raking scratches down one cheek and that there was a smear of blood on his forehead.

He moaned again and stirred slightly.

"Miles!" She loosened his tie and collar. His eyes opened. He said something she couldn't catch, then tried to struggle into a sitting position.

"Harriet," he muttered. "Saw Harriet." With Emma's help he sat up, adding gaspingly, with the ghost of a smile, "She doesn't—half—pack—a wallop." He put up a hand and gingerly felt the top of his head. He looked at his fingers. "Blood!" he said in a surprised tone of voice.

Emma peered more closely. "The wound's not deep but it does want cleaning."

"Most extraordinary thing." Miles was speaking indistinctly, slowly, pausing between words. "I couldn't settle down—thinking of Harriet wandering somewhere—in the storm. I set out on one last search—keeping to the—shadow of the trees. Then I saw her—right in front of me. Struck me—that something about her was—different. She seemed to be slinking along and—suddenly—I was asking myself whether she might not be dangerous after all. I followed her. She went through the hole—in the hedge. Seemed to be able to—see in the dark but—I couldn't. I switched on my torch—went after her." Miles was still speaking with difficulty, the pauses more frequent. "She went round this—blasted bit of wall. I went round—this blasted bit of wall. Had—fleeting glimpse—Harriet—standing high on—masonry. Then, wham! Next thing I knew—your voice." He was silent a moment. "Did *you*—see Harriet?"

"Yes, from my bedroom window. That's why I came out." Emma sat back on her heels. "Shall I get Geoffrey to help you up?"

"Lor', no. I'm recovering—rapidly." Miles began to struggle to his feet. "Let me—hang on to you a moment. There! I'm—doing fine."

Emma looked at him dubiously. Perhaps it was the quality of the light that gave him such an extraordinary appearance. "Congested" was the word that came into her mind. As if, she thought, all his insides had risen up into his head, filling it to bursting point. Even his eyes appeared to bulge. She hoped he was not more badly injured than he appeared to be.

"You ought to go home and clean up that place on your head."

Miles laughed, an unpleasant sound. "Don't you worry. That's what I intend to do. But first I'm going to ring up our wonderfully inefficient police. Tell them my ever-loving wife is on the rampage." He sighed and put his hand up to his head. "Can't think why she should have done it," he muttered, as if to himself.

"I'll give you a hand as far as the Lodge."

Miles started. "You'll do no such thing. What d'you think I am? A weakling?"

Emma retrieved his torch, which had rolled some distance away. She helped him over the rough tangle of briar and weed. They pushed their way through the hole in the hedge. Once on the path, Miles drew a deep breath of satisfaction.

"Splendid! Now you go home to Geoffrey. Tell him Harriet's still alive—and that everything is under control. Got that? No need for anyone to worry."

Miles nodded to her farewell, winced at the sudden stab of pain the gesture caused. Then he walked off up the path, moving a little stiffly. He turned the corner and was lost to view.

Emma listened intently in case he called for help. No such call came. She went back to where she had found Miles. Against the wall was the pile of weed-covered masonry on which Harriet must have stood. She saw a brick with a dark stain on one corner. She picked it up. Miles' blood, she thought. She dropped it hurriedly.

She could only think that Harriet had struck him in sudden terror. She knew that she had an irrational fear of her husband. The need to find her seemed stronger now, not weaker.

She shone the light into the cellar. It was empty even of rats. She looked up the precariously clinging staircase and heard the floor above straining in the gale. No one, she thought, could get up there. She wondered fleetingly whether the walls would still be standing in the morning.

A floor board was suddenly wrenched off above her. It went flying past, high up, into the darkness. The elms set up an ominous creaking.

Emma decided to get back onto the path. She would make her way to the Workshop. There she would leave every light on and make short sorties into the surrounding woods until she found, or was found by, Harriet. And when she was found? They would just wait until someone came looking for them. In her heart she hoped that that someone would be Geoffrey.

She set out up the long path to the woods. The wind now was blowing in gusts. When it dropped she called Harriet's name. When it blew she battled on.

Chapter Seven

At the police station, all was ordered bustle. The enquiry into the shooting of Consuelo Buckler was proceeding. Telephones still ringing. People calling. Among the police there were also some faces strange to Finch. This pleased him, since it spoke of a force gradually returning to its normal strength.

Sergeant Lloyd, who had been on the promotion course, introduced himself to Finch. After a few enquiries as to how the sergeant had fared, Finch settled down to read the reports and the pile of telephone messages already received, Lloyd hovering over him.

Interpol had not known the reason for Justin Besson's visit to England. They had undertaken to get into touch with the police at Rennes who, no doubt, could find this out, if they did not know already.

The accounts written by the family of their movements at the Guy Fawkes party had been analysed. According to these findings Consuelo Buckler had not been seen later than nine o'clock. This accorded with Dr. Barnet's estimate of the time of death. The autopsy had shown that she had been alive when she had fallen into the lake. She had died of drowning, but would have died in any case of internal haemorrhage from the two bullet wounds.

The strong room, opened by old Mr. Judd of the firm of Judd & Son, Solicitors, had disclosed only an envelope containing copies of the wills of both Theodore and his wife—and the latter's jewel case, the contents of which were intact.

Most of the telephone messages were from people who thought they had seen Harriet, or from cranks who had some plan for her capture. There were others complaining of the modern tendency to let lunatics loose on an unsuspecting public.

Finch came to the end of the messages. He stacked them neatly into a pile. He saw that a slip of paper lay by itself. He picked it up.

"By rights, that shouldn't have come here," Sergeant Lloyd explained. "It's from an old party at Waterloo House. He's always complaining of trespassers. This time it's the light seen last night in the empty house next door, which he owns."

Finch glanced up at the sergeant. "*The* light?"

"Well, sir, it isn't the first time he's complained of a wandering light seen during the last couple of months. I've been round myself but there were no signs of unauthorised entry. No broken locks. No smashed glass. I fancy the light must come from some passing vehicle shining at an angle onto a window. Only we can't convince Mr. Dobson."

"How comes it that Mr. Dobson is about so much at night?"

"His wife had become an invalid, sir. There's a nurse who looks after her by day. At night he takes over. I understand that it was owing to her ill-health that they moved out of the big house."

Finch thanked the sergeant for his information. He ambled away in search of Superintendent Bodkin, taking the slip of paper with him.

Bodkin looked up. "We seem to be getting nowhere

fast. There was no sign of Harriet either at Philip Wheatley's flat nor at Cedric Carter's flat—or shop."

"No sign of Harriet at the Workshop either. However we have this." He laid the paper in front of Bodkin. "Sergeant Lloyd says complaints about this wandering light have been coming in for the last two months. If we turn up past reports I think we'll find they began less than six weeks ago."

"You mean someone has been keeping Harriet Buckler in that empty house?"

"I mean that she herself has been taking refuge there."

"But how would she get in? I remember that Lloyd said that there was no sign of a forced entry."

"The house used to belong to James Buckler."

"That was—what?—four or five years ago?"

"But how many people bother to take a key off a key ring when its use has vanished?"

Bodkin was silent a moment. "But if Harriet Buckler has been hiding deliberately, it must mean that she is no longer suffering from amnesia."

"Nor, in my estimation, has she done so at any time since her return."

Bodkin shifted uneasily in his chair. "Then what's she up to?"

Finch sighed. "The answer would probably not minister to anyone's peace of mind. Consider a moment. Harriet was once high-spirited, gay and greatly admired. She had everything to make her happy until that day in March when her small child was killed. She then suffered from amnesia, which supposes a complete loss of memory. She is put into a mental home and utterly abandoned by the Bucklers and hence, no doubt, by her erstwhile friends. She recovers her memory to find herself in this home. In those workhouse clothes, no jewelry, no make-up. None of the family has been to see her, nor have they written or even telephoned. Nor do they do so. She must have felt herself an outcast."

"Then," said Bodkin slowly, "the home changed hands and the Bucklers have no choice but to have her back."

"And look at her! A sullen black crow of a woman, poisoned by resentment and hatred. An alien figure, yet always within sight of the house—except when her husband wants her and she deliberately runs into the woods to avoid him."

"You might be wrong there," said Bodkin uncomfortably. "About hating them, I mean."

"Then what about Harriet Buckler's outburst of violence last Friday? Consider what forces must have built up inside her to burst out and precipitate that scene of carnage and violence. From what I heard, she would have killed Consuelo if she could have battered down the cloakroom door."

"Someone did kill her four days later," Bodkin pointed out gloomily.

"Perhaps we would know why if we could find out just what happened to Harriet that made life so intolerable that she preferred to forget everything."

"Thought we did know."

"So did I until something young Emma said concerning the time sequence of events in the Ilverstoke District Hospital. Listen. On Sunday, March 25, Harriet is carried in there unconscious. Two days later her husband breaks it to her that their child is dead—*and six days later she loses her memory.*"

There was silence for a time. Superintendent Bodkin sat brooding. "I can't help feeling," he said at last, "that this case would have seemed a damned sight less complicated if you had had nothing to do with it."

Finch was driving his own car. He was on his way to the hospital. He stopped for a moment outside the gates of Westlea Park to pick up Sergeant Hollis.

"You were right, sir," said Hollis, sinking onto the seat next to Finch. "Mr. Grant says that Mrs. Buckler went to tea with friends on the Monday. When she came back she asked him whether there was a copy of the *Gazette* in the house, since she had been told that there was a photograph of her in it. Mr. Grant lent her his copy. He had seen the photograph on the front page, taken at a charity ball held at the town hall. On the back page were what he called 'Hatches, Matches and Despatches.' The *In Memoriam* to Justin Besson had been at the foot of the column. I suppose the name caught her eye."

"She had heard it first from the expert on thirteenth-and fourteenth-century antiques as being that of the man most capable of having copied the 'Annunciation.' After all there can't have been many of them. He may well have added that Besson could not have known the purpose for which the copy had been made, since he was a man of known probity—thus putting the onus for any criminal motive on one or the other of her two stepsons."

Finch drove on. It had been as simple as that. Consuelo had reached the conclusion that Besson was dead and buried under the ruins of The Elms. She had not been able to resist the temptation of letting her suspicions be known. Her suggestion that The Elms should be rebuilt had not been made with the idea that Harriet should be confined within its garden walls. It had been a warning, a threat. An expression of her belief that if the debris of the house were to be cleared away the body of the missing Frenchman would be found.

Who, Finch wondered, had been within hearing at the time? Not that it had made any difference to Consuelo's fate. That had already been worked out to the last detail.

Finch ran the car under the trees close to where the track leading from the Workshop came out. He stepped from the car and waited. Hollis joined him. The traffic coming from one direction ceased.

"Traffic lights at the crossroads at the end of Grove Drive," Hollis shouted above the wind.

"And in the other direction Harriet could have seen the headlights of approaching traffic coming down the opposite hill. There! Where there's a space between those two houses. She only had to wait and choose her moment to cross the road. The shrubs lining the drive would have hidden her from the windows of Waterloo House as she made her way to the front door of James Buckler's old home."

They drove on. Finch enquired whether Hollis had been able to find out who had inserted the *In Memoriam* notice.

"I got onto the editor. He told me it was Cedric Carter." Hollis hesitated, then remarked, "I'd been thinking from Topham's manner these last few days that he had been responsible."

"I fancy Topham believed you were getting on a bit too fast and wasn't sorry to see you suffer a setback, but I'm willing to bet it was Carter who thought up all that business about Justin Besson."

"But I hardly know the fellow."

"I fancy you cut him out."

"With Marion?" Hollis was startled. It set up an unaccustomed train of thought, as he went back over the last year and a half. For the first time he saw his conduct as it must have appeared to others. His cursed jealousy. His idiotic whining. His sulks and frowns. What could have possessed him to treat his wife as he had done?

He became aware that Finch was speaking.

"Hollis, if you want to apply for a transfer to the Special Branch, the Superintendent will back your application."

"That's very kind of him, sir," said Hollis, with none of the delight he would have expected to feel.

"And you'd better find out if your wife is willing to go with you," Finch added with deliberate brutality. "From what I've seen you haven't given her much cause to want to do so."

Hollis roused himself from his gloomy thoughts. "I know that, sir. But if she is willing I'll see she doesn't regret it." Upon which both men lapsed into a thoughtful silence.

Emma sat in the Workshop's one comfortable chair. Young and healthy as she was, the events of the last two days were taking their toll. She had reached a stage of exhaustion where she no longer felt anything but a numb lassitude.

Several times she had gone into the woods, calling Harriet's name and flashing the light from her torch. Twice during the first half hour a policeman had called to know if all was well. The second call was now some time ago and neither man had reappeared.

She glanced at the staring face of the kitchen clock. Ten minutes past eight. She sighed and closed her eyes. She did not fall asleep but her thoughts ceased to torment her.

She was roused suddenly. Someone was banging on the front door. "Let me in," a voice cried. "Quick! Let me in! Let me in!" It seemed to express an infinity of fear.

Emma raced across the two rooms. She opened the front door. The wind, with a wild shriek, tore it from her hand, banging it back against the wall. Harriet stumbled over the threshold.

She was a scarecrow figure. Her frock was torn and muddied. Her silver-link belt had gone. Her hair hung about her, loose and wild. There was a bruise on one cheek. Her face was ghastly pale and she seemed about to faint.

Emma seized the door and forced it to close. She shot the two bolts, then turned to look at her sister-in-law. She saw with a pang of pity that at some time tears had washed a furrow down the grubby face.

"Hide me! Don't let Miles get me." Harriet's hands, timorous yet insistent, clutched at Emma's wrists, climbed up her arms, and all the time she trembled and shook while sobs broke from her lips.

"Harriet, don't!" Emma could not bear to hear such desolate sounds. She threw her arms around her sister-in-law, holding her close.

She had taken it for granted that Harriet would be softer and flabby to the touch. Instead, despite its trembling, the body she clasped was firm, even muscular. This unexpected discovery left Emma with a vague feeling of disquiet, even repulsion, for which she was immediately ashamed. She helped Harriet into one of the white chairs. By now she had ceased crying, more from exhaustion, Emma thought, than from any effort of will.

"I've fallen," Harriet said in an exhausted, toneless mutter, so that Emma had to lean forward to hear what she was saying. "I've caught my frock on the brambles. The zip has jammed so that I'll never be able to get it off. I've lost my belt—and somewhere I nearly lost my life."

Emma listened with astonishment. It was the longest, most coherent sentence she had ever heard from Harriet. "Was that when you hit Miles with a brick?"

Harriet gave her a fleeting glance from under drooping lids. "How did you know?"

"I found him unconscious." As she spoke Emma remembered the pale slits of eyeballs. Had Miles only been pretending so as to arouse her sympathy? And yet—why should he have thought it necessary? He must have known he had it. "I wanted to help him get home but he said he could manage."

"Only he didn't go home. He's still searching for me. He'll come here. You'll see." Harriet fell to shivering again in a convulsion of overstrained nerves.

Emma could not decide how much, if any of this was true. And Harriet herself seemed to have changed. She looked familiar and yet not familiar. All the known features were there yet she appeared smaller, darker— and denser. Emma could not have explained what she meant by this final word and yet it seemed apt. Suddenly she realized that still one other change had taken place.

Harriet no longer suffered from amnesia.

Bemused, Emma went into the other room. She brought back a bowl of warm water, soap and a towel. She waited a moment, then, since Harriet made no attempt to wash her hands or face, Emma began to do it for her.

"When did you get your memory back?" she asked, in a purposely conversational tone.

"Months ago." Harriet spoke so readily that Emma thought the question must have taken her by surprise. "The doctor at the mental home," she added hurriedly, "didn't care one way or the other. He only wanted the money." She took the soap and bent over the bowl, washing her hands with so feverish an air that Emma could not but think of Lady Macbeth.

"I would have told you," Harriet muttered, "only there were the others—and it wasn't all pretence. I hated them—particularly Miles. I wanted to see him squirm. I knew just what to do. That ridiculous walk. These awful frocks. My aversion for him—he can't bear not to be liked. I was delighted, too, to see what dissension Consuelo was causing in the family. When she'd beg Dad to have me shut up I'd laugh to myself, thinking that I was just the kind of person who ought to be shut up—" Her racing words came to an abrupt halt. She let the soap fall unregarded onto the floor. She said, almost in a whisper, "Only—these last two days I've been so frightened."

"You mean—Consuelo?"

"It began before that. Miles kept calling as if he must find me. Hurrying into the woods as if he were looking for me. Only—once he was there, he'd stroll about as if he had all the time in the world. Or he'd sit smoking. Once he saw me. He waved—and he grinned—horribly." Harriet shuddered.

Emma suppressed a sigh. She knew none of that was true. Hadn't she spent hours with Miles searching for Harriet? "So what did you do?"

"I hid in James' old house. The one the Dobsons bought."

"But it's all locked up."

"I still have a key."

"I see." Emma's voice was colourless. Her sister-in-law was rapidly becoming someone she did not know. There seemed a world of difference between Harriet of the broken heart and mind, as Dad had once called her, and Harriet, the impostor, the spiteful, even perhaps the murderous.

"Don't turn against me, Emma. You're the only friend I've had here. I've always realised that."

"There was Dad."

"Dad was only my friend as long as it didn't affect Miles—" Abruptly Harriet stopped speaking.

The wind had fallen suddenly. Now, in the succeeding lull, Emma fancied that she heard a soft, cautious sound. Someone was moving about outside. Glancing at her sister-in-law, she saw that Harriet sat frozen. Her eyes wide, terrified, and oddly vacant, were fixed on the door.

The ring handle turned. Very quietly and slowly it turned. The door creaked as if someone pushed it from the other side. Then, with the same silence and stealth, the ring handle fell back into place.

Listening intently, Emma heard footsteps moving lightly away, slipping a little on the fallen leaves.

Small moaning sounds broke from Harriet's lips and her body grew tense. The bruise stood out on the extreme pallor of her face. She clutched at Emma's arm. "Promise you won't let him in. Promise," she whimpered.

"I promise," Emma answered, almost automatically. "No one can—"

Harriet's grip tightened. "Hush!" she said, and went back to her dreadful listening.

The footsteps returned, openly now. The voice, Miles' voice, sounded calm, ordinary. "Emma, are you there?"

"Yes, I'm here."

"Let me in."

"I'm not going to let anyone in."

"Emma, don't you start acting queerly." Almost she could hear the exasperated sigh accompanying the words. "These last few weeks you've seemed the only sane female in a mad world."

Emma was tempted to open the door. Miles' voice was so familiar. So—pleasant. She glanced at Harriet and the impulse died.

"I'm not letting anyone in."

"Like Garbo, you want to be alone? Rather hard on Geoffrey, isn't it?"

Emma recalled her last conversation with her husband. "He doesn't care any more. He wants me to go back to France."

"Heaven give me patience! He just wants you safely out of this nasty mess."

Emma's heart seemed to give a great bound. "Miles, is that really true?"

"Of course it is. Now open the door."

"No. I can't do that."

"Which means you have my mad wife there. I was afraid of that when I found the front door locked."

Emma said nothing.

"Emma." Miles' voice was rough. "I'm only thinking of you."

"That's why I'm keeping the door bolted."

"Meaning you think you're in danger from me? You flatter me. Well, if you want to lock yourself up with a homicidal maniac, that is your lookout. But just ask yourself where you think Harriet has been this last hour. Ask yourself what else she has done."

Emma was conscious suddenly of a small but definite reaction on her sister-in-law's part. From where she stood she had not seen what it had been. She heard only the sudden whisper of her frock as Harriet, with some quick movement, broke her frozen stillness.

"If you'd done what you said you were going to do," Emma retorted, shaken yet dogged, "the police would be here by now. There'd have been no need for me to lock myself in."

"I admit I didn't actually telephone them, but I did speak to a constable I met on my way back to the Lodge. He promised to pass on my message but he wasn't very hopeful about getting any result. It seems that there's a bit of a riot on in West Ilverstoke. He and most of the others were being withdrawn from here to cope with it. However I did go round to the Small House to see Geoffrey."

Emma's heart leapt. "What did he say?"

"He didn't say anything. He wasn't there."

Emma's heart jerked in dismay. "Where had he gone? To The Grange?"

"No. I tried there. My own guess is that he went out hunting for you."

"But—he'd come here."

"Now don't panic. I didn't see him but that doesn't mean that anything has happened to him—although I must admit there was every sign that he had left home hurriedly. Cold cup of coffee. A sheet of paper, the typing broken off in midsentence—"

Emma's mind was in a ferment. Her heart sickened as she saw in her mind's eye a picture of Geoffrey wounded, crawling painfully on hands and knees, lying dead or dying under some bush. How or why, she did not ask. A sob broke from her.

"That won't help," said Miles. Adding impatiently, "Have some sense, girl! How can we talk with the door between us?"

Emma's mind was full of thoughts of Geoffrey. She would have opened the door but for her promise to Harriet. "Please go away," she called, in a voice that shook. "I'm not going to open the door to anyone but the police."

Miles gave a short laugh. "Have it your own way. Only don't say I didn't warn you. That is, if by morning you are in a fit state to say anything."

Both women heard his retreating footsteps. They sounded for a moment and then were no longer audible.

"What's he doing now?" Harriet whispered through ashen lips.

"I suppose he's on his way home," said Emma, picturing him walking away up the ridge. She wished she were with him.

Harriet seemed to shrink still further into herself. "He's still there," she said dully. "Searching for a way in."

Emma looked at her sister-in-law impatiently. "I'll have a look from the window in the next room."

She switched off the lights and stared out into the woods. She had expected to see a light bobbing away in the distance. Instead there was only darkness. The room seemed now to be oppressively silent. There was about it a muffled air of suspended life—an acute sense of waiting. Only—waiting for what?

Emma became aware that Harriet had crept to her side. "I'm frightened," her sister-in-law whispered. And the light slanting in from the outer room showed her eyes bright and unreasoning, like those of a wild animal.

They stood there, listening, their dark clothes lost in the shadows. Only the pale blur of their faces remained and the sound of their hurried breathing as they stood poised on the brink of panic.

"I'll turn on the light and draw the curtains," said Emma, in a voice she forced to be steady. "And you can sit in the one comfortable chair." She got a cushion. She threw it on the floor and seated herself on it. "Tell me what happened between you and Miles at the hospital?" she said, for something to talk about. "Geoffrey and I have often discussed it but we never actually knew."

Harriet told her.

Emma listened, aghast, sickened. Everyone had agreed that Harriet had adored her little son. She could not imagine her making up such a phrase as "a hunk of raw meat" in describing his lifeless body. No, there she must be telling the truth. "The beast!" she said with conviction. "The cruel beast! No wonder you lost your memory."

Harriet shook her head. "It wasn't that," she said dully. "It was seeing the old man—dead—lying there on the carpet."

Emma stared. "Lying on what carpet?" she asked, bewildered. And, unbidden, the thought slipped into her mind that perhaps Miles had been right in part. Harriet was mad—only, of course, not dangerously mad.

She was speaking again. "At home. The Elms. I went back there that Easter Monday."

"But—I thought you didn't want to come back?"

"That was Dad's idea. Best not, he said. I knew he

meant best for Miles—but I wanted to see Bunny's nursery just once more. And it was quite easy to get away from the hospital. I just dressed and walked out. I knew the maids would have gone to the fair and I hoped that Miles would be at The Grange. Anyway I decided to risk it.

"I stood at the bottom of the garden and looked at the house. It seemed to be empty, so after a few moments I plucked up courage and let myself in by the front door. As soon as I was inside I realised that I was not alone. Someone was down in the cellar. Who it was or what they were doing, I didn't know. I hesitated for a moment, then I tiptoed towards the stairs. The door into the drawing room was open and, on impulse, I walked in."

The hoarse, muttering voice ceased. Harriet was staring, wide eyes fixed on some dreadful vision only she could see.

"And then?" Emma prompted her.

"Then I saw him—an old man lying in a great pool of blood. *And I knew him*. At least, I'd seem him two years before." Harriet drew a deep, shuddering breath. When she spoke again it was in a more ordinary voice. "It was after Dad wrote to say that he was getting married. We'd never thought of that happening and Miles was furious. He swore he'd pay Dad out and, of course, we did need the money. We took the carved ivory 'Annunciation' from the cabinet—"

"Oh, no!" Emma's eyes were enormous.

"You're shocked? Well, you asked me." Harriet's voice had an almost hostile tone. It startled Emma.

"Of course," she said hurriedly, "I've never had much money so I've never missed it." She did not want to seem a prig.

Harriet looked in two minds whether to say anything further. When she did continue, it was in her old flat bitter voice. "We took the car over to Brittany and called at a house near Rennes. Miles went in alone. When he came out he had this old man with him. A tall fierce old man with a tuft of beard and large, bare sandalled feet."

Monsieur Besson! And the strangeness of this reappearance widened Emma's eyes and caught her breath. Strange, too, that but for a whim on her part, his replica would even then have been staring from across the room, eyes watchful, smile derisive.

"I knew then what was happening in the cellar."

Emma's skin was crawling. "Someone was digging a grave."

"*Miles* was digging a grave," Harriet corrected sullenly. "You're certain?"

"I saw him—staggering down the passage towards the cellar door with the old man on his back. I'd heard him coming up from the cellar and I'd hidden behind one of the drawing-room curtains."

Emma stifled a sigh. Harriet seemed still to be in a nightmare world of her own making.

The wind, rising suddenly, shook the window frames and shrieked around the corners of the house.

Harriet began to shiver again. Her fingers plucked restlessly at the material of her frock. She said suddenly, "You don't know what it's like seeing someone who has been murdered. Revolting—and yet pathetic. They don't look human any more. Not even when you had known them quite well before it happened."

"But you didn't know Monsieur Besson except by sight."

"No, I didn't know him," Harriet agreed hastily. Abruptly she fell silent. Sat shivering, shaking, her teeth chattering.

Emma, looking at her, wished that there was something to drink. Even the beer she had finished earlier that day would have been better than nothing. "I'll just clear up. Then I'll make some tea." She was not a tea-drinker, being more accustomed to coffee, but it seemed a nice ordinary thing to be doing on this most extraordinary of evenings. Besides, it might do Harriet some good. Tea and sugar for shock, she said to herself.

There had never been much china kept in the Workshop. Just two mugs, two plates and a teapot. She began to wash up. Behind her Harriet was at it again—a compulsive talker after her long silence. Her muttering voice tore at Emma's nerves.

"It's dark, so you can't really see. You bend down and there's that awful smell again, like being at the butcher's, only worse. You put out a hand and touch cold flesh. Colder than anything you could have imagined—"

Emma went into the front room to fetch the bowl of dirty water. Harriet's words didn't make sense. Unless, of course, she had been speaking of Consuelo's death—and then the bit about the butcher didn't apply.

The bowl was on the floor beside the leather chair into which Harriet had collapsed. Emma bent down to pick it up.

The floor seemed to open beneath her feet. There was a churning high up in her throat while wave after wave of nausea swept over her.

On the side of the chair low down was a long smear of fresh blood.

Emma stood staring at the telltale stain. So Harriet hadn't been speaking of the death of the Frenchman. Nor yet that of Consuelo. There had been another death. Harriet had brought the blood from it back on her frock.

An echo of Miles' pleasant voice echoed in Emma's ears. "Ask yourself where you think Harriet has been this last hour. *Ask yourself what else she has done.*"

An appalling realisation came to Emma. She had been at some pains to lock herself in with a murderess.

Chapter Eight

The Ilverstoke District Hospital was a sprawling building, half concrete, half glass. Finch and Hollis were
shown into a small room on the ground floor while Dr.
Harrison, the casualty officer, was sent for.

He proved to be a cheerful snub-nosed young man. A
stethoscope hung round his neck, and his hands were
thrust into the pockets of an immaculate white coat.

"Of course I remember," he said in answer to a
question from Finch. "Not only because Mrs. Buckler
was a real good-looker. Not because her name is in the
newspaper this morning, but because of something that
happened here and which made a real sensation at the
time. Still, that's not my story."

He perched himself on the edge of the centre table.
"As for her injuries, Mrs. Buckler got off comparatively
lightly. She had a nasty bump on the head and was
unconscious when they brought her in. Her child?" He
shrugged, screwing up his face in a grimace. "The poor
little devil had practically to be scraped off the wrecked
side of the car. There simply wasn't anything we could

141

do to make him even recognisable to his father when he came to identify the body. But perhaps you're not interested in that?"

"I'm interested in everything you can tell me about Mrs. Miles Buckler. I keep hearing that she was responsible for her mother-in-law's death. Yet that death was advantageous to other members of the family and I'm worried in case I am being offered a sacrificial lamb. This," Finch added, "is, of course, in confidence."

Dr. Harrison nodded. "Naturally," he said. He slid off the table. "You'd better see Dr. Gregson. I don't think he has gone off duty yet and Mrs. Buckler was his patient."

He took them up in a lift to the third floor. He left them in the passage while he went to talk to his colleague. A few minutes later he returned. "Come on in," he invited. "Dr. Gregson can give you half an hour."

A pleasant voice came from the room. "Half an hour? You must be joking."

Dr. Harrison grinned. "Well, it's back to the salt mines for me." He wrung Finch's hand. "A pleasure to have met you." He nodded to Sergeant Hollis, stepped into the lift and was carried from sight.

Dr. Gregson was a sandy-haired man of no more than average height, fit and wiry. He had a thin face, very clear blue eyes, and an air of competence and dependability that must have been reassuring to his patients.

"What exactly was it you wanted to know?" he asked when he had settled the two detectives in chairs on the opposite side of the desk. "Of course I have read the newspaper account of Mrs. Theodore Buckler's death, but if you want an assessment of her daughter-in-law's mental state you have come to the wrong man."

"No, I've got that taped," Finch answered. "What I want to know is whether anything happened here that could account for Mrs. Miles Buckler's amnesia?"

Dr. Gregson nodded. "Now, that's not so difficult. It stemmed, I imagine, from her husband's visit. He had asked particularly that he should be the one to break it to her that their child was dead. And, since his wife had not been badly hurt, it was only two days later that I rang him up and told him that he could go ahead. I gave it as my opinion that she already suspected the truth. He thanked me quite pleasantly for phoning and said that he would come round right away."

Finch found himself attending more narrowly to the doctor. He knew that Miles Buckler had upset his wife, but Dr. Gregson's tone of voice seemed to suggest something more than this. "And so?"

"Sister Bates showed Mr. Buckler into the private room where his wife was. She reported to me that she was pretty certain that I was correct in my suspicions that Mrs. Miles knew that her baby was dead. When she had seen her husband she had stretched out her arms to him and the tears had poured down her face. I remarked that, when I had seen the patient in the next room, I would go and see how they were coping. Mrs. Miles, I said, might not be in any danger from the accident but a crying jag would not do her any good."

"And how were they coping?"

Dr. Gregson's face hardened. "I'll tell you. I hadn't been a couple of minutes with my other patient when the whole private wing was startled and horrified to hear the sound of shouting and shrieking coming from Mrs. Miles' room. I rushed into it, followed by Sister Bates. Fortunately she is a levelheaded and sensible woman. She closed the door and stood with her back to it so that no one else could get in.

"The scene was extraordinary. Miles Buckler was on the bed, one knee holding down his wife's legs while, with his hands, he pinned down her elbows so that she was powerless to move. His face was not a foot from hers and he was shouting, 'Bunny is now no more than a hunk of raw meat. That's what you've done to my son. A hunk of raw meat, I tell you.' His wife was petrified, like an animal caught in a trap. She was staring up at him and I'll swear she didn't even realise that she was screaming."

"Miles Buckler says that since he saw his wife two

months ago and realised what he had done, he has been
overwhelmed with remorse."

"That fellow? Nonsense! I have never seen such
hatred on a human countenance. It would take a lifetime to dissipate, let alone nineteen months."

Said Finch, "I'm pretty certain this isn't generally
known, not even in the family."

"That would have been the work of the old man—
Theodore Buckler. I sent for him and told him what had
happened. He was shocked. Genuinely shocked, but
his main preoccupation was that nothing of the affair
should be known outside the hospital, of which I may
say he was a very generous supporter. He was also a
man of considerable influence in other quarters. This
place was humming with the story but not a word of it
ever appeared in any newspaper, either local or national."

"I'm told that Mrs. Miles was forbidden all visitors.
Was that your decision or Theodore Buckler's?"

"The decisions concerning patients are all mine. And
Mrs. Miles was in a pitiable state, given to tears and fits
of trembling. Terrified that her precious husband would
come back."

"And when did she lose her memory?"

"That came later—and a queer business it was."
Anger had drained from Dr. Gregson's voice. Now he
sounded no more than interested and a little puzzled.
"Easter Week was upon us and, as you can imagine, it
is a quiet time here, with as many patients as possible
going home for a long weekend. The same applies to
the private wing. For those who remain, there is no loss
of attention but there are far fewer people about and
therefore less supervision.

"Mrs. Miles had expressed no wish to spend the
weekend anywhere but here, yet on the Monday afternoon about four o'clock she was found by Matron on a
chair on the first-floor landing. She was dressed, ready
to go out, and was clutching her handbag. She was in a
curious state, remote, calm, physically very cold. When
Matron asked her where she was going she answered in

a dull flat voice, very different from her usual one, that she had only wanted to see her home."

"And then?"

Dr. Gregson looked at Finch. "That's the extraordinary thing. When I came on duty at seven o'clock I went to see her—*and she didn't know me from Adam*. In the course of a few hours she had passed from a state of mild shock to one of total amnesia."

When Finch and Hollis returned to the car, the two-way radio was spluttering. Hollis picked up the mike. A voice informed him that Superintendent Bodkin wished to speak to Chief Inspector Finch. A moment later the Superintendent was there. Demanding why Finch didn't take a police car in a Christian manner, so that there was someone to answer the radio.

"Tell me your news," he ended grimly, "then I'll tell you mine."

Finch did so. "And there you have the explanation of that entry in Miles Buckler's diary. Harriet came back and he was all set to embark on the double plan of revenge that was to see his stepmother dead and his wife either dead or consigned to Broadmoor—probably the former."

"And the cause of Harriet's amnesia?"

"I think the two nurses left in charge that Easter Monday lied. I think that when Matron found her, Harriet *had* been home. The only thing I can't decide" —Finch's voice was very soft and drawly—"is whether the amnesia arose because she came on the murdered body of the Frenchman or because she had murdered him herself."

"If it was the former, we must hope Miles doesn't find out. He'd have to kill her then."

"He has found out. He found out last night when Emma and Geoffrey told him that his wife haunted The Elms because she had an idea that something horrible took place there and that she wanted to remember what it was."

"From what you say it doesn't sound as if she had her wits about her."

"I think Miles ain't the only one filled with hatred," Finch answered. "And I wouldn't like to say which of 'em, Harriet or Miles, is going to come out on top. She *may* be out of condition, but not so long ago she must have been in perfect physical shape. For all we know, she may have been doing a toughening-up course in the woods. And she always was a good shot. As to which of 'em bagged Consuelo, your guess is as good as mine."

"Or which of them will go next," said Bodkin's gloomy voice.

"How about arresting one or both?"

"In this weather?" The Superintendent's exasperated roar vibrated in the mike. "If I had five times the number of men at my disposal I still might not catch either of them. And I haven't even the men I had an hour ago. There's a near riot going on in West Ilverstoke. Students rampaging about in protest at what they're pleased to call our harassment of Cedric Carter. And Sergeant Lloyd has been watching the Dobsons' empty house for the last hour, but not a sign of anyone."

Finch waited for a moment for the Superintendent to simmer down. Then he enquired if there had been any news from Interpol.

"Yes, they came through not fifteen minutes after you'd left." There was a curious reluctance in Bodkin's voice. "Said that the Rennes police had told them that early yesterday morning Philip Wheatley had been making the same enquiry as we had about Besson's reason for coming to England."

"And what has Wheatley to say about that?"

"Nothing," Bodkin answered. Adding, and his voice was uneasy, "Fact is, we haven't been able to find him."

Finch was conscious of a quick stab of dismay. "Now that I don't like! Meet you at Westlea Park," he said.

Emma stood for a moment in a trance of horror, her eyes on the telltale streak. And then from the other room, there came a sound. Harriet, with a light furtive tread, was moving about. Emma's eyes turned to the doorway but it remained blessedly empty.

Her thoughts raced, pursuing each other up one blind alley after another. You must be calm, she told herself. Calm and swift. Walk to the front door. Unfasten it, then run. Run for your life.

She remembered suddenly that Miles had said that Geoffrey was missing. Her fear for herself was swallowed up in a great swelling of fury. She marched back into the other room.

Harriet was standing by the centre table, quite still. The knife, Emma thought. She's got the knife. But it was still on the plate beside the fruit cake and anyway it did not seem to matter. She marched round the table to Harriet's side.

"Who else is dead? Who is lying out there in the dark—colder than anything you could imagine?"

Harriet looked at Emma, her face deliberately blank. "I don't know what you mean."

"There is blood on the side of the leather chair. It must have come off the hem of your frock."

The effect of this was as electrifying as it was unexpected. Harriet gave a wild cry. She seized the neckline of her frock, tearing at it. "Take it off! Take it off!" she cried hysterically. "Oh, get it off me!" She threw her arms around Emma's unresponsive body.

"Whose blood is it?" Emma asked stonily.

"Philip's. It was Philip Wheatley's." Harriet's arms slid down her sister-in-law's stiff body as she sank to her knees. "But I didn't kill him. I swear I didn't." And then, "Oh, get me out of this frock, please, please!" She fell silent, her face pressed to Emma's skirt, through which she transmitted the shudders of repulsion that shook her from head to foot.

"Philip?" Emma could not help the sudden leap of her heart to hear that it had not been Geoffrey. Then she remembered Philip as he had been only a few hours back. Standing in that very room, happy, triumphant. His long servitude ended. And now he was dead. She looked down at her sister-in-law searchingly.

"I didn't kill him," Harriet declared, answering that glance. "I haven't killed anyone. Not the Frenchman.

Not Consuelo. Not Philip. Not even Miles, although I could have done so." She looked at Emma distractedly. "I could see that you were wondering what I was doing at the table when you came in but I was only eating a slice of cake. I was so hungry. I haven't eaten since breakfast time. That was how Miles caught me. I was on my way to Westlea Park to get some food." Perhaps she felt the stiffening of Emma's body as mentally she repudiated the truth of this explanation. "I know it wasn't the direct route to the house," she went on in a weeping voice, "but that way I could keep among the trees almost the whole time. Only it wasn't any good. Miles was waiting for me in the ruins. He must have found out I often went there."

Emma felt the stirring of remorse. She banished it fiercely. "You must have been prepared for that. You were always there."

"I know! I know! I wanted to frighten him. To let him know his life was in my hands—only it wasn't." Harriet got awkwardly to her feet. Stood staring dumbly at Emma.

"Well? Get on with your story." It couldn't be Miles who was the murderer. It couldn't. It must be Harriet—or—or someone else.

"Miles lifted me off my feet," Harriet began obediently. "I kicked him and he hit me." She put a trembling hand up to the bruise on her cheek. "I scratched his face and he let me go, only I couldn't escape. I was trapped between the two walls. He kept moving slowly forward and I kept moving back. At last I was against the wall. Miles laughed then, and said he was going to hold my head under the water in the fountain until I was dead. Then, when it was all quiet, he'd come back for me. He would drop me into the lake, weighed down by the statuette of Bunny which Dad had given back to him after the fire. He said it would be a fitting end. He said weighed down, it would be days before I'd become bloated enough to come to the top. That long before that, the fish in the lake would have eaten my face away."

Harriet looked at Emma through her tears. There was no encouragement to be seen there. Tears are cheap, Emma was thinking. Consuelo taught me that.

"All the time Miles had been talking my hands had been moving behind my back, feeling for a loose brick." Harriet's voice now was toneless, flat, her old bitter voice. "I found what I wanted. When Miles sprang at me I hit him. He dropped and I ran." She went on drearily, "I seemed always to be running, falling over roots, catching my frock, my hair. Soon I couldn't run any longer. I crawled in under a large bush and I think I must have fainted. When I came round I decided to try and get as far as James' old house. I crawled round on all fours under the bush so that I'd come out at the nearest point and suddenly there he was. *Philip!* He'd been there with me all the time. Miles must have dragged him there by his feet. He was wearing a raincoat. It was all rucked up above his head and it was full of blood from his broken skull. I touched his face. Not to feel if he were dead—I could see that—but I had remembered that he had loved me once. I had tormented him but I'd let him make love to me too. Then I scrambled to my feet. I was running again. The next thing I remember was seeing the light here and you letting me in."

Yes, I let you in, Emma thought. She did not know whether she believed anything of Harriet's story. It did not seem to matter much. If Harriet were a maniac killer then obviously she, Emma, would not be allowed to escape from the Workshop alive.

"I'll get some water and wash the hem of your frock," she said quietly. She fetched the bowl and refilled it. Kneeling at Harriet's feet, she worked stoically away as the water grew pink. She watched without fear or pity as her sister-in-law seemed to be attempting to shrink into herself, little cries of repugnance bubbling from her lips and distorting her mouth. Emma felt nothing at all.

"Thank you, Emma," Harriet whispered at last. "Thank you very much."

"If only I could believe you," Emma said desperately.

"I know." Harriet looked at her sadly.

Emma saw that she looked desperately ill and—and decidedly odd.

"I'll make that tea," Emma said, as she had said earlier. She scrambled to her feet.

"Wait!" Harriet's voice was urgent. She felt for her pocket, feverishly yet gingerly as if she feared to find it full of blood. She produced a crumpled envelope. "I found this lying by the lake. It must have—have fallen from Consuelo's hand. I'd forgotten I had it."

Emma took it. The writing, she thought, was familiar. She drew out a letter. It was dated simply Tuesday.

> *"Dear Aunt,"* it read: *"You were right. I only wish that I could have been in so that we could have rejoiced together. Since Uncle is not to know, I have no reason not to go out on a totally unimportant errand for him, so have left this with the porter. From what the police at Rennes said, it seems obvious that Justin Besson did copy the original 'Annunciation' and came over with the intention of borrowing back his work for a one-man show. Why Miles should have killed him remains a mystery. Incidentally, knowing that the doors of the Lodge are never locked, I went in last night and found Miles' passport. He and Harriet went to Brittany on 15 May 1970 returning three days later. This seems to me pretty conclusive. See you at the party tonight."*

It was signed "Philip."

Emma looked at Harriet. "That poor old man." She tried to give the letter back to Harriet, but she shrank away from it with such obvious distaste that Emma was forced to keep it.

"Was he ever found?"

"Missed, but not found."

"He's here somewhere, isn't he? Cedric Carter's copy?"

"Yes, in the other room. Do you—do you want to see him?"

Harriet shook her head. "I've never forgotten him."

To both of them he seemed to be present. To Harriet, it was the papier-mâché figure. To Emma it meant Monsieur Besson, the man with the watchful gaze, the derisive grin.

"And now Consuelo and Philip are dead. It doesn't—" Emma broke off, silenced by something in Harriet's appearance. She stood quite still, lips parted, eyes vacant. It was as if every faculty but that of hearing had been suspended.

"What is it?" Emma asked, whispering.

"Someone is outside."

"Miles? He's back?"

"Listen!"

Now both women heard it. A curious scraping noise, very soft and strange. Suddenly Emma recognised it for what it was. Someone—Miles—was climbing up an outer drainpipe to the attic room.

The trap door! It was not open—but then it was not bolted either.

Emma raced for the stairs. As her hand fell on the bolt she heard, very softly, someone land on the attic floor. Desperately she tugged at a bolt stiff with disuse, as footsteps sounded moving stealthily towards the trap door.

The bolt creaked into place.

The two women froze while Miles tried first to lift, then to lever up the door. There followed a pause—for a minute? Five minutes? An hour? Emma found that the palms of her hands were wet.

Miles stamped on the flap, over and over, a hideous, terrifying noise. It shook, it shuddered but it did not give way. Then, as abruptly as the stamping had begun, it ceased.

The footfalls sounded again, openly this time. They crossed towards the window. Emma thought she could

hear Miles sliding down the pipe, but knew it could be
only imagination. The wind had risen and was howling
about the building once more.

She looked at Harriet and felt that somehow she
must distract her attention—unless she wanted her to
go out of her mind again.

"Tell me about Consuelo being shot," she heard
herself say ineptly, and had to struggle against a strong
desire to burst into loud and uncontrollable laughter.

Harriet seemed to find nothing odd in the enquiry. "I
was watching the fireworks," she said, in the voice now
of utter exhaustion. "I was at the far end of the lake and
had pushed my way into a little clearing right at the
water's edge. Then suddenly someone spoke quite close
to me. I recognised Consuelo's voice. It said, 'So I have
the last laugh after all.' Then her voice changed. I heard
her cry out, 'No, Miles, don't—' And then I heard the
sound of shots and someone moving away, snapping the
branches as they went. I waited a minute, trembling
and frightened. Then I pushed through the bushes
separating me from where Consuelo had been. I saw
her lying on her back. Perhaps she wasn't quite dead. I
don't know. I saw the letter lying there. I picked it up."

"When Consuelo was found, her head and shoulders
were in the lake."

"Miles must have gone back and made certain."

"You didn't think of going for help?"

"No. I had realised by then that I had stepped into a
trap. That I was to be suspected of killing Consuelo. I
turned and ran. My cloak caught in a bush but I didn't
wait to disentangle it. I didn't stop until I found myself
in James' old house. Oh, it was cold without my cloak.
So cold—" Harriet yawned suddenly, cavernously.

There was silence for a time. Emma was lost in
thought.

"D'you know I expect that was why James and Viv
never went to see you. Not because they didn't want to
but because they thought that you might have been
back to The Elms and seen Monsieur Besson. They

were afraid that seeing them might help to bring your memory back."

"I know." Harriet sounded drowsy—or was she faint? "Viv was always trying to pump me. To make certain, as she thought, that I knew nothing—"

Emma, looking at her, saw that she had fallen into an exhausted sleep. It was not a peaceful sleep, for soon she was moaning, muttering words that were unintelligible.

What a desperately long night it was going to be! Emma thought. Only it would not be a whole night. If no one else came, Miles at least would be back. Even without knowing that Harriet had the letter he could not afford to let her live—even if he had not hated her.

She thought how odd that was. All that pretended affection. Only, when one came to think of it, the masquerade had occupied barely six weeks. She realised too—and it still had the power to shock her—that all anyone had ever heard of Harriet's condition had come from Miles. Her suicidal tendencies, her supposed theft of the pistol. And she never had come down that night after her attack on Consuelo.

The minutes passed. In a queer way, Emma thought, it was worse with the curtains drawn. Outside, anything could be happening. The thought brought with it an eerie sense of danger. It seemed for a moment as though she had only to creep to the windows and draw back the curtains to surprise the face of her brother-in-law pressed against the bars.

The room which she had known so well had become as strange and unreal as the stage setting for an unknown play. A play as nightmarish in its inception as the row of figures standing straight and still and eternally smiling in the further room, just out of her sight. The thought came to her that perhaps the Frenchman had stepped out of line, drawn by the story of his own end and the presence—

The wind was not as strong now. It muttered ambiguously in the chimney. It rattled the window frames as if with an impatient hand. The clock ticked on, although now time had lost its meaning, become only something shown on its bold, white face.

And then the killing of Philip, which must have happened just after he had left her, began to run, slow-motion, through her mind. The manner of his death tore at her nerves, as did Harriet's uneasy mutterings.

"This won't do," she said aloud, and was frightened at hearing so strange and hollow a voice. She decided that she must find some occupation. She would go on making the second dummy, although she knew that she would never come here again to work—nor, if she could help it, for any other reason.

She went to the cupboard to get some newspapers. Suddenly she stiffened, then whirled around. A small furtive sound had come from the back room.

The Frenchman, she thought, appalled. He's coming out.

She listened, but the sound was not repeated. She heard only the rising note of the wind and her own heart thumping.

Suddenly she heard it again, slight and secret as it was. She stood motionless, even her breath suspended.

The sound came again. Changed a little now. Creak, thump. Creak, thump, just as Cedric had laughingly predicted.

Emma slipped out of her shoes. She walked on silent stockinged feet across the floor. She opened the door into the back room with a sudden jerk, expecting, in some far corner of her mind, to find herself face to face with Justin Besson, called back to some ghastly form of life.

He was where she had placed him. The row of figures stood unmoving, eyes and smiles fixed. Then a sound, a strange, low, whining sound brought her heart into her mouth.

Cautiously she lifted a corner of a curtain. Cautiously she looked out across the Frenchman's shoulder. The next moment she had bitten back a startled cry; for not twelve inches from her own face was that of Miles. His eyes were wide and blind-looking. He wore a fixed skull-like grin and in his hand he held a hacksaw.

With it he had sawn through two of the bars. He was now at work on the third.

Emma let the curtain fall while wave after icy wave of terror flowed over her. She crept back to the other room, closing the door silently behind her. She put on her shoes, then knelt beside Harriet, calling her name softly but urgently.

She had hoped not to startle her sister-in-law but Harriet jerked herself upright, staring wildly around for the danger, never totally forgotten, even in sleep.

"Don't make a sound," Emma whispered. "We shall have to change our plans. Miles is using a hacksaw to file away the bars of the small room. We shall have to go."

Harriet's face turned ashen. "I couldn't," she moaned. "I just couldn't."

"Then I shall leave you," Emma declared. "You can lock yourself in this room and I'll try and get the police here in time."

"No!" Harriet grabbed at Emma's sleeve. "You can't leave me."

"I can and I will." Emma felt a perfect brute as she said it. "I have something to live for, if you haven't."

Harriet scrambled to her feet. "What are we going to do?" she asked in a quavering voice.

"Your part is simple and practically foolproof. I shall stand in the doorway of the back room and if the sawing stops I'll make a diversion to keep Miles at the window. Meanwhile you must hide in the woods. Just turn to the left or right when you're out of the house and crawl in somewhere." Emma added apologetically, "It's all I can think of. You see—you haven't really much run left in you."

Harriet nodded. "I'll do what you say." She looked so small, so vulnerable, determined and yet sick with fear, that Emma's heart melted. She put her arms round her and kissed her warmly. For a moment they clung together.

Emma led the way into the front room. She climbed onto one of the display tables and drew the hangings over the door. "If you get behind the curtains by the cupboard and work your way round, you can get out without the light betraying you. And draw the door together after you, but don't shut it." She smiled, hugged Harriet again. "Be seeing you," she said, and, stepping back so that she could hear the whine of the hacksaw, watched her sister-in-law moving towards the front door, undulating behind the hangings and so letting herself into the night.

Left alone, Emma seized the figure of the Welsh Witch and tore off its skirt, which, fortunately, was on an elastic. She put it on, then covered her bright hair with the black chiffon scarf. She had no intention of attracting Miles' attention but if he did follow, it might be as well if he thought that she was Harriet.

She paused for a moment, thinking uneasily that the whirring hacksaw had changed its note. Then she let herself out of the front door in the same manner as Harriet had done.

Here she met with an unexpected setback. After the brightly lighted rooms, the darkness seemed impenetrable. Shivering, her heart thumping so loud that she feared Miles must hear it, she stood there.

Gradually her eyes accustomed themselves to the moonlit night. Trees came into view. The familiar path appeared before her.

She gathered up her long skirts and ran, ducking under low tossing branches and keeping a lookout for any fallen ones, skidding occasionally on moss or leaves.

Finch's car left the Ilverstoke District Hospital with the velocity of a bullet. It wove in and out of the traffic, which fortunately was light.

The wind banged on the windows and boomed against its roof. Shops, supermarkets and petrol pumps flashed past. The car came to the residential area and now there was nothing to each side but fancy ironwork gates

and walls hiding pseudo-Georgian buildings, and the
road running pale and almost empty before them.

It came to Grove Drive where, above the empty
howling of the wind, rose the sound of the crashing of
branches. The car drew up under the trees. Finch and
Hollis sprang out, running along the rough track, stumbling a little as the moonlight struggled down in uncertain deceptive patches.

They saw the Workshop, the light pouring from its
windows and open front door. They saw a window from
which not only the bars and glass had gone, but where
the very window frame itself had been shattered, jut-
ting out now at odd angles with an uncomfortable
suggestion of having been the object of a wild, mindless
fury.

"Straight on," Finch ordered. If anyone were still in
the Workshop, then they were dead and beyond help.

Emerging from the trees, they saw that there were
two people running in front of them. One was unmis-
takably Miles and, for a moment, Finch was deceived
into thinking that the fleet-footed leading figure was
that of Harriet Buckler. Then he realised that the
voluminous skirt clothed an altogether longer-legged
young woman. He realised, too, that if Miles could
mistake Emma for his wife, then Harriet must still be
alive.

He shouted to Hollis to go back and find her.

Emma glanced back and saw Miles with the figure of
the Chief Inspector in pursuit. So I was right, she
thought. Miles must have been on the point of breaking
through when I left. She thought too: If only he doesn't
shoot me—if only I can keep far enough in front so that
he can't break my neck— Her flying feet seemed scarcely
to touch the ground. Her skirt, far from impeding her,
caught the wind like a sail, helping her on.

A sudden shot whistled by her head, making her run
still harder. Now Miles was no longer her brother-in-
law and Geoffrey's half brother. He was the murderer of
Consuelo, Philip, and the Frenchman, cruel, swift and
infinitely menacing.

She wondered frantically whether it would have been wiser to have made for the Small House.

The next moment she was certain that she should at least have taken a different route; for, hurrying round a corner, came Geoffrey.

Seeing Emma, he paused in patent relief, tinged with some astonishment at her appearance. The next moment he was reeling back as she launched herself at him, throwing her arms round his neck and twining her long legs about his.

Geoffrey, taken completely by surprise, tried in vain to prise her off him. "Emma, damn it! Let me go! Have you gone mad?" But Emma clung with the tenacity of a boa constrictor and the elusive agility of an eel.

"He shan't shoot you," she panted. "He shan't. I won't let him."

By now Geoffrey had seen Miles approaching, the police, in the person of the Chief Inspector, behind him. He saw the white, furious face of his half brother, the skull-like grin, the pistol clasped in his hand.

"Emma!" Geoffrey's voice was a desperate command. Finding that she took no notice, he swung round, presenting his back as a target for Miles. "Now will you let go," he said in a grim voice.

For answer Emma let out a banshee-like wail. She unwound her legs and arms and fell thump in a sitting position on the ground. Geoffrey winced slightly on her behalf, then turned to face his half brother. He saw then what Emma and Finch had already seen.

One of the great elms was falling.

"Miles, look out!" he cried. "For God's sake, look out."

The roots of the tree tore loose with a grinding noise. With a fusillade of snapping and cracking, with a noise greater than any wind, the great bole crashed down. There was a long dying rumble, then all was quiet.

Just when Geoffrey and Emma had thought Miles safe, a branch seemed to reach out and pin him to the ground. They ran forward, clambering over the fallen trunk and over or under its many branches until they

came to the one that held Miles prisoner. Finch, they
saw, was already there. One glance was enough to show
them that no number of human hands would shift that
branch.

"Keep still, dear old boy," Geoffrey said. "We'll get
William and his cross saw. We'll have you out in no
time."

Miles seemed to have difficulty in focussing his gaze.
"Don't leave me." Great beads of sweat were breaking
out on his forehead. Emma, holding back her tears,
knelt beside him, wiping his forehead with the hem of
her long skirt.

Miles saw her. "Emma—always—quite a girl." A
spasm of pain wracked him. "So silly," he whispered.
"All to no purpose. At the last—couldn't catch Harriet."
As if some secret message as to his condition had come
to him, he gazed at Geoffrey, a curious urgency in his
face.

Geoffrey bent forward to hear the faltering whisper,
uncaring that Finch had done the same. "I killed
Consuelo. Dad—couldn't take it. Just killed Philip—the
upstart." He was silent a moment, gathering together
his failing faculties. "Began with—Frenchman. He ac-
cused me—cheat and—liar. Made me—mad. Mad—
perhaps that's the answer—"

Geoffrey took his half brother's free hand. His eyes
were full of tears. "Don't try and talk," he urged. "Just
take it easy. You'll be all right."

Miles made a supreme effort. He squeezed Geoffrey's
hand in affectionate response. "All right for what?" he
whispered with the travesty of a smile. His eyes glazed
over. His mouth fell open. A small trickle of blood ran
down his chin.

This time it was Geoffrey who seized Emma in a
convulsive clasp. They clung together, trying to comfort
each other, while Finch, looking up, saw Superintendent Bodkin and Sergeant Topham, alerted by the
pistol shots, appear hurrying in the distance.

Geoffrey Buckler detached himself from Emma, although he still held her hand. "What did Miles mean

about Philip?" he asked hoarsely. "He didn't—?" His voice drained uncertainly away.

It was the Superintendent who answered him. "I don't know how much your half brother knew but Mr. Wheatley and Mrs. Theodore Buckler had been working together. They were perilously near to finding out what had happened to the Frenchman who disappeared on the third of April, last year." Adding briefly, "We haven't been able to find Mr. Wheatley since he left The Grange."

"He's dead," said Emma impetuously. "Harriet hid from Miles—" She remembered. "Harriet! Someone must look for her."

"It's all right," said Finch soothingly. "Sergeant Hollis has gone to find her. Your brother-in-law can't have done so or he wouldn't have been chasing you."

"You were going to say something about Mr. Wheatley's whereabouts," Bodkin reminded Emma.

"Harriet hid from Miles by crawling under a bush. I don't know which bush, but Philip was already there, only"—Emma threw an anxious glance at her husband—"only he was dead."

"Dear God." Geoffrey passed a shaking hand over his face. "I'd better telephone James." He paused for a moment, still holding Emma's hand. He looked at her as if he were about to say something. Then he pressed it in mute—apology, appeal? He turned to trudge wearily away, back to the Small House.

Emma blinked eyelashes suddenly wet. She felt down the front of her frock and produced the crumpled envelope. "Harriet picked this up when Consuelo was shot. She must have dropped it when she fell." She glanced swiftly at Finch. Read his expression aright and passed the letter to Bodkin. "I didn't want to give it to you in front of Geoffrey. He's upset enough."

Bodkin read it with an expressionless face. "Very much what Interpol told us," he said with superb assurance.

Finch meanwhile had picked up the pistol which lay

close to Miles' open hand. "Jammed," he said briefly. He looked at Emma. "You were lucky there."

"In fact," said Bodkin, "you and your husband have been lucky all round. There'll be no trial now, only an inquest."

"I expect that will be a comfort later on," said Emma politely. "I think now I'll go and find Geoffrey."

She walked away, the long skirt of the Welsh Witch's dress flapping.

"Pluck. That's what she's got," Bodkin declared. He turned to Finch, lowering his voice. "I'll tell you something. I've been in touch with Mr. Judd." He explained the terms of Theodore Buckler's will with obvious relish. "His wife's estate goes to relatives back in South America. In fact the only one who hadn't made a will is that chap there." He jerked a thumb downwards towards Miles. "So his widow gets the lot. She'll be a rich woman."

"Let's hope Miles can't know. He might come back and haunt her," Finch murmured.

The police driver from the car which had brought the Superintendent was hurrying towards them. "Message from Sergeant Hollis, sir." He caught sight of the dead man. He started, gulped and turned pale. "The Sergeant found Mrs. Miles. He's taken her back to the police station. She is weak but unharmed," he said, averting his gaze.

"Right!" Bodkin's relief was obvious. "I'll get back there. Topham, you come too." He added to Finch, "Not a bad idea to get Dr. Russel to hide Mrs. Miles away in some West End nursing home where the press can't get at her."

"I think the point about the press will have to be stressed. After all, Harriet Buckler has just come out of a home."

"Point taken." Bodkin leant nearer to Finch, his eyes narrowing into two mirthful slits. "Matter of fact," he said in a confidential tone, "give me a nice fraud case. This one has been a letdown, hasn't it? All the work we put in. Up practically all night. You, hard on the heels of the murderer. And what happens? A bloody great tree comes down on him and we might all just as well have stayed at home." He walked away, his shoulders shaking with silent laughter.

Finch now was alone. There was a pause that was strangely peaceful. The wind had dropped completely, as if satiated by the havoc it had caused. The moon, riding high in a clear sky, cast a peculiarly cold and dreamlike clarity over the scene so that everything appeared unreal—and the dead man the most unreal of all.

Finch looked down on him and wondered just how far the word "eccentric" had been stretched to describe the dead man's mother.

The police surgeon arrived to pronounce the obvious, that Miles Buckler was dead. He gave it as his opinion that his rib cage had been crushed. That there must be grave internal injuries. Like Bodkin, he seemed slightly amused and went away remarking it was the damnedest thing.

Hollis arrived, driving, with evident enjoyment, his superior's car. His eyes widened as he surveyed the scene. He reported that he had almost reached the Workshop in his search for Harriet when she had appeared from among the trees, tottering unsteadily towards him. She had clutched his arm, muttering, "Emma! Save Emma!"

"And then," said Hollis, "before I could make a move she had passed out at my feet. But by the time I got her back to the police station and had fed her, she was well enough to make a statement to the Super." Hollis went on to give Finch its gist. It was in the main what Harriet had told Emma earlier that evening. "So when it became essential that Miles Buckler find his wife, sir, it was already too late," he finished. "She had hidden herself away in the empty house. Still, I don't suppose it ever occurred to him that he wouldn't catch her eventually." Finch recalled Miles as he had seen him at the Lodge that morning. A man with a face no less grey than his dead one. "It occurred to him, all right. Not surprising when one considers that probably he had been up all night searching for her. What did not occur to him was that his wife had recovered her memory and, when put to it, was as wide awake as he was."

"And yet," Hollis remarked, "if he could have brought himself to visit her in the mental home, someone would probably have told him. It seems it was no close-kept secret."

"It was his hatred that destroyed him. Once she realises its strength, everything becomes plain. His fear that I had run Harriet down and so destroyed his plan. His grief, not at the destruction of his house, but at its necessity."

Hollis nodded, "Probably blamed her for that, too, sir."

"Yes, plenty of blame going around. Pride too. And what came of it? Consuelo is dead. Theodore, Philip Wheatley, this chap here—and Justin Besson."

"D'you think the Frenchman guessed what Miles Buckler had done?"

"Must have done—if he asked to see the original 'Annunciation' and the copy together once again."

They fell silent as they heard the sound of a car approaching.

James Buckler appeared and Geoffrey came from his house to meet him. Then followed a long vigil as the two half brothers, ashen-faced and silent, awaited the arrival of the powerful crane which was to lift the fallen tree. Finch did not envy them their thoughts.

When it was all over, he overheard a single bitter comment from James. "Odd," he said to Geoffrey. "I used to warn Miles that one of these days he'd do something he wouldn't be able to live down. I never dreamed that I'd be the one left to try and do it."

Three days had passed. Finch and Hollis were once more in the overgrown grounds of The Elms. The fallen tree had been sawn up and taken away. The twisted flattened frame of the fountain and a broad swathe of destruction showed where it had lain. The L-shaped walls had gone and now added to the great pile of debris which had once been three floors and a roof.

Finch and Hollis were perfectly content: Finch because he was about to return to New Scotland Yard; Hollis because he and Marion were happier than he could have imagined possible.

"Let's see the plan Grant helped you make," said Finch.

"He thought the Frenchman would have been buried near the foot of the cellar stairs, sir," Hollis answered, handing it over. "Otherwise Harriet Buckler would not have heard her husband."

"The main staircase must have been—here." Finch had climbed onto the great mound of rubble and charred wood.

Hollis joined him. "And the Frenchman," said he cheerfully, "would be about here, sir"—he stamped his foot—"under this little lot."

"From where," said Finch, "you'll have the job of getting him out. When the bulldozer has done its work, as the expert you'll be the first to be given a spade—unless, of course, your transfer to the Special Branch comes through in time to save you." He found a couple of tiles to keep the plan flat. "Bet you you'll discover only a naked body. Miles would never have risked leaving the Frenchman's distinctive clothes on him." He added with professional interest, "Wonder if the fire assessors found any foreign oddments in the wreckage."

Hollis, looking past Finch, remarked, "Seems as if we've got visitors, sir."

First Emma and then Geoffrey came through the hole in the hedge. Emma was wearing a coral-pink shirt blouse and a grey-flannel suit designed to suit lanky girls. Her soft bun of hair, bristling with hairpins, was in process of undoing itself. Geoffrey looked haggard and desperately tired. They appeared, if not actively happy, then at least utterly content in each other's company. They stood looking up at the two detectives.

"And I was just congratulating myself that at last we

had the place to ourselves," Geoffrey remarked. "Is this visit official?"

"I'm sorry about it, but the Frenchman must be found," Finch answered, climbing down from his high perch. "We hope to have the bulldozer driving more or less straight for the cellar door."

"From what I remember of the house," Geoffrey commented, "I should say it was just about under where your sergeant is standing."

"Where the pile of rubble is highest?" Finch sighed. "I was afraid of that."

"I believe Besson had no family," said Geoffrey somewhat stiffly. It was awkward talking about a man whom a member of one's family had killed.

"He had a sister married to a small-time farmer. They hadn't communicated with each other for over thirty years, although they lived quite near each other. She inherits his not-inconsiderable fortune and wants him buried in the family plot."

"My brother doesn't intend to live in Westlea Park so, no doubt, you'll be dealing with the National Trust in future. Harriet means to give them this ground. It should"—Geoffrey's voice was heavily ironic—"round off the property very nicely."

"How is Mrs. Miles?" Finch enquired.

"Looking much more her old self," Geoffrey answered.

"That's because she's got Walters." Emma favoured Finch with one of her wide smiles. "Isn't it fantastic? She went and saw Harriet the very next day at the nursing home. As soon as Harriet is free they're going to the South of France for the rest of the winter."

Finch recalled the favourable impression the lady's maid had had on him. "D'you know," he said slowly, "I think that should work very well."

A silence fell. The wind blew a little and the remaining elms creaked. The shadow deepened on Geoffrey's face, and Emma slipped her arm through his.

"And how is Mr. Carter?" Finch asked. His own opinion was that that young man should be in prison awaiting trial for incitement to riot. Unfortunately Carter was not the kind of man on whom unpleasant retribution was apt to fall. A view only strengthened by Emma's reply.

"I know Cedric doesn't deserve it but he's making a fortune. He's got the effigy of the Frenchman down at his shop and it's drawing crowds. There have even been one or two bus loads running to West Ilverstoke to see it. They can have their photograph taken arm in arm with it and they pay enough." Emma added in a low voice, "I've left off being afraid of it because in a way it saved my life. I never would have gone to see what was making that queer sort of sound if I hadn't thought it was the Frenchman moving about."

"And if most of the police hadn't been in West Ilverstoke at the time, putting down a near-riot Cedric had engineered, you would never have been in danger," Geoffrey pointed out.

"Well, at least Cedric was upset about that."

"*Cedric* was upset? How d'you think I felt when I found you weren't in the house?"

"How did you find out?" Finch asked curiously.

"I'm usually pretty good concentrating on my work. I'd even managed it that evening, when suddenly it came to me that I hadn't heard anything of Emma for hours."

"But why should you?" Emma demanded. "I never interrupt when you're working."

"No, my love," said Geoffrey, smiling at her, "but you do tend to sing, whistle, and even swear about the house."

Emma looked conscience-stricken. "But I only swear in French. That doesn't count." She appealed anxiously to Finch. "You wouldn't call that *swearing*, would you?"

"I'd say it was more educational," Finch assured her solemnly.

ABOUT THE AUTHOR

MARGARET ERSKINE has written over a dozen mystery novels in the classical tradition—carefully shaped and plotted and highly literate. They include *The Family at Tammerton, No. 9 Belmont Square, The Woman at Belguardo, Case with Three Husbands,* and *Harriet Farewell.* The Erskines are a Lowland Scots family connected with the Stuarts by many inter-marriages and, from Bannockburn to Culloden, they fought on every battlefield of Scotland. Miss Erskine was educated by governesses and the vast resources of her father's library in South Devon. She now lives in London.

CATHERINE AIRD

For 15 years, Catherine Aird's mysteries have won praises for their brilliant plotting and style. Established alongside other successful English mystery ladies, she continues to thrill old and new mystery fans alike.

WHODUNIT?

Bantam did! By bringing you these masterful tales of murder, suspense and mystery!

Masters of Mystery

With these new mystery titles, Bantam takes you to the scene of the crime. These masters of mystery follow in the tradition of the Great British and American crime writers. You'll meet all these talented sleuths as they get to the bottom of even the most baffling crimes.